AS144127

D1421177

or excellence in public service
Dumfries and Galloway
ries, Information and Archives

Dumfries a
LIBRA
Information and Archives

Dumfries DG1 1JB
.bs&i@dumgal.gov.uk

Daughter of Evil

When Jake Probyn hauled up outside the Circle F ranch, he was looking for work and not trouble. But trouble in the shape of the boss's daughters and the foreman, Ransome, was what he found. Things got worse when the old man died and left the ranch equally to his daughters.

Then there were back shootings and range fires with one daughter going missing. There was trouble galore waiting for Jake.

The Drowned Valley on Circle F land certainly had its own eerie story to tell.

Daughter of Evil

H.H. Cody

A Black Horse Western

ROBERT HALE · LONDON

ISBN 978-0-7090-8723-6

Robert Hale Limited
Clerkenwell House
Clerkenwell Green
London EC1R 0HT

www.halebooks.com

Typeset by
Derek Doyle & Associates, Shaw Heath
Printed and bound in Great Britain by
CPI Antony Rowe, Wiltshire

ONE

Jake Probyn hauled on the leathers of his horse
outside the yard of the Circle F ranch. The yard
was empty. The door of the bunkhouse at the top
of the hill was open. A lazy blue line of smoke
crawled into the empty blue sky.

There was no one around. His hand hovered
over the butt of his .45. He caught the movement
of the curtain and stepped onto the veranda. The
door opened a mite and the barrel of a Winchester
poked through it.

'There's no need fer that,' he said in a peace-
able voice.

'I'll decide what there's a need for,' the girl's
voice said. 'Who are you and what do you want?'

Probyn stepped back a pace, his hand moving
away from his gun.

'Step off the veranda an' into the sunlight where
I can get a better look at you.'

Probyn stepped off the veranda and took another look at the yard. The door opened and the girl came onto the veranda.

Probyn looked her over. She was a right good-looking girl, even with a Winchester in her hand.

'My name's Jake Probyn an' I'm lookin' fer work.'

'I'm Sarah Fleming. OK, Jake Probyn,' she said looking him over like he'd looked her over. 'Just wait here while I get my pa.' She went back in the house and closed the door. Probyn wondered where all the hands were.

After a few minutes the door was opened, and she came out with her pa.

'Sorry about the welcome,' the old man said. 'But my daughter she kinda thinks I can't look after myself.'

Probyn said nothing. The old man had a head of white hair and a livid scar that ran down from his hairline to his jaw.

Squinting at Probyn, he looked him over, like Sarah had done. 'What can I do fer you?'

'Folks in town reckon there's work goin' here,' Probyn said.

'Folks'd be right,' the old man answered. 'I figure they didn't tell you we had trouble at the Circle F?'

'No, they didn't,' Probyn answered.

'Well we are an' it's gettin' a damn sight worse all the time,' said the old man.

'Pa wants you to know what yer gettin' into. If you want to you can ride out with no hard feelin's.'

Probyn had guessed that there was something wrong, just a feeling in his bones.

'No, I won't be ridin' out,' he said slowly, and saw the look of relief on their faces.

'I'm Ralph Fleming, the owner of this spread,' the old man said with a sound of pride in his voice.

Probyn looked round again, and for the first time noticed the air of neglect that was settling over the place.

'Sarah tells me yer name is Jake Probyn. Pleased to meet you,' Fleming said, holding out his hand and taking a step forward.

As he did so, he stumbled. Probyn and Sarah took a step forward to catch him before he fell.

'I'm obliged,' Fleming said, when he had recovered. 'Sarah, take Jake up to the bunkhouse an' show him where he can put his stuff.'

'OK, Pa,' she said. She went to put her hand under her pa's arm, but he shrugged her off.

'I kin manage,' he snapped, glaring at her.

'Sure, Pa,' she said, and followed him into the house.

Probyn waited in the burning sun for her to come back. When she came out, she was still holding the Winchester.

'OK, let's find you a bunk.' She pointed him up the hill.

7

As they walked she was silent for a moment. Then, 'You ain't from hereabouts, are yuh?'

'No, I ain't got anywhere I can call home. I'm a drifter, I guess you'd call me,' he said, watching her taking the heads off some weeds with the Winchester. He waited for the next question.

It came. 'Where are you from originally?'

He could have lied, but he didn't. 'Mason's Landing.'

'I can't say I've ever heard of it,' she said after a silence that had seemed to stretch.

Probyn felt a wave of relief.

'Somethin' the matter?' she asked him as they reached the bunkhouse door.

'No,' he said more sharply than he had intended.

He started to unfasten his bag from the back of his saddle. Sarah had gone into the bunkhouse. He followed her in.

'The crew left in a hurry,' she said, seeing him looking round the place.

'What kinda hurry? The place looks like it's bin hit by a storm.' He laughed. There was gear everywhere.

'Night riders in Drowned Valley saw a fire buildin' up. Ransome got everybody out there, an' they ain't back yet. Toss yer stuff on the bunk under the window. The fella who had it last won't be usin' it again.'

'He quit?'

'No, a hunk of lead from a Winchester quit for him.'

There was something in the way she said it that made Probyn think he might not have been the only one.

Sarah walked to the window and looked down the trail. He saw her fiddling nervously with the gold brooch she had in her shirt. It was a plain gold circle with the letter F in it.

'Pa bought me an' Debbie one each after Ma died,' she told him when she saw him looking at it.

Probyn followed her gaze and saw riders galloping in the direction of the ranch house.

'That's the crew. I'm going down to see what happened. Ransome will be up later.'

When she had gone out, Probyn tossed his bag on the bunk and rolled a stogie. Then he heard footsteps coming along the veranda. The crew clumped into the bunkhouse. They looked pretty beat up.

'Looks like ol' man Flemin' found himself another sucker fer a target.' The speaker was a short, squat individual.

'Knock it off, Loomis, the fella ain't even got his gear out of his bag yet.'

'Just think a fella ought to know what he's lettin' himself in fer,' Loomis said.

Probyn watched the two men. Like everybody in

the bunkhouse, they seemed plumb worn out.

Loomis dropped into his bunk and put his hand behind his head. His face was dark with smoke, and his eyes red-rimmed with exhaustion.

Probyn looked up from his bunk. 'What's bin goin' on, fellas?' he asked.

'Hell's come to the Circle F. That's what's bin goin' on,' Loomis said. He got up and built himself a stogie. 'Range fires. Back-shootin's. Life sure as hell's got dangerous round here.'

'If there's bin back-shootin', why hasn't the boss got the law onto it?' Probyn asked him.

'Say Mister-new-round-here,' Loomis said. 'The boss has bin seein' the sheriff since it started, an' it ain't got him nowhere. Jim Diamond is in somebody's pocket but not ol' man Flemin's. Say, what's yer name?' Loomis flicked the ash off the end of his stogie and went across to Probyn.

'Jake Probyn,' Probyn said taking the proffered hand.

Loomis took it, then stepped back, studying Probyn's face.

'Must be thinkin' of another fella,' he said at last.

Probyn felt relieved as a shadow crossed the door, and the crew stopped talking.

'Where's the new hand?'

'Guess that's me,' Probyn said, turning to face the newcomer.

'I'm Clem Ransome. I'm the foreman round here.' It was the voice of a bully.

'Jake Probyn,' Probyn said, not liking what he saw.

'OK, Probyn. Keep yer nose clean an' do as yer told. An' don't go botherin' Mr Fleming or Sarah. If you've got anythin' you need to know come to me. Savvy?'

Ransome looked at the others in the bunkhouse. 'Miller, Loomis, git some grub an' meet me outside the stable. I've got a job fer you. Bring the new fella. Take him up to Drowned Valley. Got that? Make sure everythin's OK.'

'The hell, Ransome. We've bin out there all night. Give us a break.'

'Give us a break,' Ransome said, mimicking Loomis's voice. 'Either git up to Drowned Valley or draw yer time.'

'Yeah. OK, Ransome,' Loomis said wearily.

Ransome turned and left the bunkhouse. Probyn watched him go down the path to the house. Then, he stopped to talk to a girl who had just come out of the stable. At first Probyn thought he was talking to Sarah. Then he realized the girl was a mite younger.

'Sarah's sister, Debbie,' Loomis said handing him back his makings. 'Her an' Ransome are pretty close, an' I don't think the boss knows.'

'I don't think he'd like it much,' Probyn said.

'The fella doesn't seem to like you too much, but I'd say he was gettin' on pretty well with Debbie.'

'That Ransome don't like anybody too much. Can't figure where the boss found him, unless it was under a stone behind the livery.'

Probyn smiled. Ransome and Debbie quit talking. Ransome headed to the house. Debbie went into the livery.

'Let's git some chow,' Loomis said. 'Then we can get down to Drowned Valley.'

When they had been served they took their grub outside and sat on a bale of hay.

'You fellas not finished yet?' a voice from behind them said.

Miller, who had been dozing with his hat over his eyes, sat up and brushed himself down.

'Yeah, we're just about through,' Miller said.

'Then git down to Drowned Valley, an' check things out,' Ransome snarled.

Miller and Loomis headed for the livery to get their horses. Probyn's was still outside the house.

'Just what is this Drowned Valley?' Probyn asked Miller as they hauled up that way.

A spooked look came over Miller's face 'A couple of years ago some settlers were headed on up to California. It was late in the season so they figured on spending the winter in the valley up ahead. Only they didn't tell any of the folks round here. Built themselves a few timber huts, and

settled in fer the winter. The place is real treacher-
ous. The snow melted real early, an' the water
came barrellin' out of the mountains. Drowned
them all. Over a hundred people, includin' kids.
Folks say on a winter night you can hear them
bawlin' fer their mummies an' daddies.'

'Aw, stow it, Fred,' Loomis said. 'Yer turnin' the
fella green.'

The men rode on in silence until they reached
the Drowned Valley. From the high ground Probyn
could see the mouldering ruins of the shelters that
the settlers had built, and the blackened grass. On
two sides the mountains rose up almost vertically.
Probyn looked the place over; he had to admit that
it had a spooky feeling about it.

'Why do you reckon Ransome sent us out here?'
he asked them.

Loomis answered him. 'See that narrow valley
over there,' he said, pointing to the opening
between the mountains. 'Somebody's bin sending
riders through to drive off Circle F cattle. Guess he
wants to see if anybody's bin through last night or
early this mornin' while we were out seein' to the
fire and make sure the fire was out.'

They rode their horses down to the valley floor.
For a while the three men scouted the place.

'Just some old tracks,' Probyn said after half an
hour. 'A couple of days old at most, I'd say.'

Suddenly a hunk of lead cut the air, and

13

Loomis's hat flew off. 'Damn it,' he spat.

They gigged their horses into some cover.

'Guess they're over near them shacks,' Probyn yelled, hauling his Winchester out of the saddle holster. He levered a round into the breech. He brought the stock up, aimed for the flash of light among the shacks and loosed off a round. Loomis and Miller also started sending some lead back, and soon a fierce fight had started.

There were about half a dozen of them, Probyn reckoned, and they showed no sign of backing off. A piece of lead had grazed Loomis's head, and the blood was running pretty freely down his face.

'You'd better git to the Circle F an' git some help up here,' Probyn shouted across to him. 'Me an' Miller'll cover you.'

Loomis scrambled to his feet, and wiped the blood away from his eyes. He pulled himself into the saddle and galloped away.

The snipers among the shacks showed no sign of easing up. Pretty soon a heap of shell cases lay at the feet of Probyn and Miller.

'Looks like they're gonna rush us,' Probyn shouted across to Miller, who was loading up his Winchester again.

He had seen the men getting mounted and starting to head their way. They rode hard out of the shelter of the shacks, and barrelled on in

Probyn and Miller's direction.

The gap started to close as Probyn's Winchester misfired. He tossed it away, and reached for his .45. It was a fairly long shot for a handgun, but he held it out in front of him at arm's length. He chose the lead rider, who was coming on pretty hard, also holding his .45 at arm's length. Probyn squeezed the trigger. The .45 bucked, and spat out the lead. The gun flew from the rider's hand, and he grabbed his shoulder. His horse bucked and hesitated. Probyn could sense the hesitation in the others.

He heard a yell. The lead rider turned his horse and the other five riders followed him back to the shacks. Probyna saw them riding beyond the shacks, and out of sight. He and Miller got up, and checked their guns.

'Wonder what that was all about?' Miller asked.

'Dunno,' Probyn said. 'You've bin here longer than I have.'

'Things have bin goin' from bad to worse fer a while now,' Miller said.

'What sorta things?' Probyn asked, checking the .45.

'This used to be a peaceful part of the world. Then steers started gettin' run off, hands started gettin' back-shot. Last night was bad. Big fire over yonder.' He pointed in the direction of the shacks. 'There's some good grazin' land in that direction.

15

Then last night, the whole thing went up like a torch.'

'What do you reckon caused it?' Probyn asked, handing over the makings.

'Don't rightly know. The place has bin hot an' dry, so I guess that might have caused it.'

To Probyn he didn't sound all that convinced. Before he could think on it, the sound of approaching horses made him look round.

'You boys bin havin' some trouble?' Sarah asked Probyn,

'Nothin' too serious,' Probyn said, reloading his .45.

'Any idea who they were?'

Probyn shook his head. 'I'm new round here, so I don't know all the local bad men.'

Sarah laughed. 'Let's git back to the ranch. Have you seen Ransome any place?'

Probyn shook his head.

TWO

Ransome sat on a rock, and watched as the rustlers came back.

The *hombre* with his bandanna wrapped round his hand hauled on the leathers and dragged his horse to a halt right in front of Ransome.

'They got some fella down there who can shoot. You didn't tell us about that, Ransome.' he said angrily.

'You ain't gettin' paid to come squawkin' to me,' Ransome snapped.

'If that fella goes on shootin' like the way he has bin, yer gonna have to give more money,' came back the answer.

'Maybe I'll just get somebody else,' Ransome snarled.

'Where have you bin, Ransome?' Sarah asked the foreman when he got back to the ranch a few hours later. 'Pa's bin askin' fer you.'

Ransome felt the suspicion in her voice. Maybe she was smarter than he realized, and that would make her dangerous. Sarah watched him. 'You'd better git up, an' see what Pa wants.'

Ralph Fleming sat at his desk going over the ranch accounts. In spite of it being broad daylight he had the lamp on full.

When Ransome knocked he turned it down.

'Come in,' he said over his shoulder.

He heard the door open, and the clump of Ransome's feet on the carpet.

'Yuh wanted me, boss?'

'Yeah, Ransome.' Fleming turned to look at his foreman. 'I guess you heard about the shootin' at Drowned Valley?'

'Yeah, I heard about it from Miss Sarah,' Ransome said quickly.

'So where were you when all this was happening?' Fleming growled.

Ransome looked round for an answer, then he saw the papers on Fleming's desk.

'I went to see Mike Redding about them horses he sold us,' he said.

'I was just looking at this bill for the horses,' the old man said straightening the papers.

'The bill is out by a hundred dollars.' Ransome said quickly.

'An' it ain't the only one,' Fleming said angrily.

'I ain't seen the others.' Ransome said. 'I wuz

gonna leave them to Miss Sarah.'

'In that case I'll deal with it myself. My daughter has enough to do,' Fleming told him. 'I ain't exactly happy about the way yer runnin' things, Ransome. Them rustlers are gettin' away with a heap of stock. I've built this ranch up over the years. I've fought Indians, renegades, an' plain ol' fashioned outlaws. Nobody's takin' this ranch off me or mine. Got that, Ransome?'

'Yeah, boss,' Ransome said sourly.

'See this?' Fleming said, fingering the scar along his face. 'Got this from the same bullet that killed my wife. Do you know what I'm sayin'?'

'Sure, boss,' Ransome said.

'OK. Just watch how you run things from now on or I'll git somebody who can. Now git out.'

When Ransome got outside his face was burning.

Under his breath he cursed the old man, and headed up to the bunkhouse.

'You ain't lookin' so good,' a familiar voice said from the livery stable.

Ransome looked round the yard. Seeing nobody around, he went inside.

Debbie Fleming threw her arms round his neck and kissed him square on the mouth. Ransome let it linger, then pulled away.

'What's the matter with you?' she asked in a sulky voice. 'You had enough of me already?'

Ransome looked at her. 'No, it ain't that. Only it ain't gonna look so great, is it, if somebody comes walkin' in an' sees us like this?'

'I guess yer right,' she said. 'What did Pa want?'

'He ain't happy about things,' Ransome said.

'Sounds like he's gettin' suspicious.'

'That's what I figured,' Ransome told her.

'We gonna let him ruin our scheme?'

'Don't look like we can do anythin' else,' Ransome said.

'Hell,' she said, suddenly flaring up. 'I've spent all the time I want to spend on this ranch and in this part of the country. I want to go where it's civilized. You and me are going to sell it, and go away like we planned all along.'

'What have you got in that pretty little mind?' Ransome asked, an inkling of what she was going to say starting to cross his mind.

'Pa's had more than his share of life. Pa's an ornery cuss, so there's no sayin' how long he's going to live. Then there's sweet little Sarah, but we can figure a way of dealing with her later.'

'An' you reckon its time to do somethin' about it.'

'It's hardly a crime. I don't expect you've noticed. His eyesight is getting worse. He'll just have an accident. Maybe fall downstairs. Could even be a blessing. No more pain for Pa.'

'I think yer right,' Ransome said, stroking his

chin. 'I'd better get goin' up to the bunkhouse to see what them three I sent to Drowned Valley gotta say. See if they can point the finger at any of Maitland's boys.'

'You go an' think about it. See what you come up with.' Debbie kissed him lightly on the cheek.

Ransome went up to the bunkhouse, leaving Debbie in the stable. After a while she walked down to the house. The straw shifted at the back of the livery, and a figure pulled himself to his feet, and brushed the straw out of his hair. He watched as the girl disappeared into the house.

'Looks like pay-day's come early,' he said to himself in a happy tone of voice.

After Ransome had spoken to Probyn and Miller he left the bunkhouse.

Probyn watched him go to the corral for his horse. He watched him saddle up and ride out. It had been his plan to follow him, but Sarah had given him and the boys a job over in the south meadow, to round up some cattle there.

A few head had strayed onto the Circle F spread through a break in the fence. Maitland ran the Broken Brand ranch, next door to Fleming's spread.

Probyn and the boys saddled up and headed that way. Miller found the break in the fence, and they went to work fixing it up.

After half an hour Miller stopped working and

pointed to four riders coming in their direction.

'We got company,' Miller said as the riders got within hailing distance.

' 'Bout time you boys came an' fixed this fence up. Your beeves have bin comin' over an' eatin' at Mr Maitland's expense.' The speaker was a swarthy man with a sly face and a tied-down gun.

The other three riders ranged alongside him. They were looking for trouble.

'Yeah,' Miller said, in a placatory way. 'Mr Fleming don't want no trouble with you or anybody else, Spalding.'

Spalding, the foreman of the Broken Brand, slipped out of the saddle and came over to Miller. Probyn pushed Miller out of the way. He flicked the thong over the hammer of his gun, and blocked Spalding's path.

'I wouldn't want to shoot a fella with a hurt hand,' he said, pointing to the bandage that covered Spalding's hand.

'Don't worry about my hand, hurt or otherwise. Me an' the boys can take care of you without too much trouble.'

'Spalding,' one of his boys said, as Spalding took a step closer to Probyn.

'Yeah, what do you want, Riley?' Spalding asked, impatiently.

Riley said something in Spalding's ear. Spalding looked towards Probyn.

'You sure about that?' Spalding asked.

'Yeah. Saw him in Dodge. He's the fastest thing that carried a gun,' Riley said quietly. Spalding lost some of his colour.

'OK. We'll let it ride. Just git that fence fixed up, an' keep them animals off Mr Maitland's land.'

Spalding turned and signalled the others to get back in their saddles. They rode away, leaving Miller and Loomis looking surprised.

'What was that about?' Miller asked Probyn.

'Can't rightly say,' Probyn lied.

None of the others looked as if they believed him.

'Just let's get on with mending this fence,' Probyn said.

Spalding and his boys rode back to Maitland's ranch.

'We got trouble, boss,' Spalding said to Maitland when he came out onto the veranda.

'What kinda trouble?' asked Maitland.

'Fleming's bought himself a gun. Don't look like it's gonna be so easy from here on in,' Spalding told him.

'Who's this gun Fleming's got himself?'

'Fella called Jake Probyn,' Spalding replied.

'I've heard of him,' Maitland said. 'It ain't in Fleming's nature to bring in outside help.'

'No, it ain't,' Spalding said, 'but we've seen him, large as life.'

'Don't do anything right now. Let's see how this fella behaves. Might have to bring in a man of our own, if he's that good.'

When Probyn and the others had fixed up the fence, they headed back to the Circle F.

THREE

'I'm goin' into town,' Probyn told Miller. 'If anybody asks where I am, you don't know. OK?'

'Not in any kinda trouble?' Miller asked.

'No, no kinda trouble.'

Probyn rode into town and hauled up outside the sheriff's office.

Jim Diamond looked up when Probyn walked in. He pushed the papers he had been looking at to one side.

'What can I do for you?' he asked.

'I'm a new hand up at the Circle F,' Probyn began. A look of irritation crossed Diamond's face.

'More trouble?' Diamond asked him.

'Not exactly,' Probyn said. 'What can you tell me about what's been goin' on over there?'

Diamond scratched his head. 'It's more a case of what's not bin goin' on.'

'I got the gist of it from Sarah,' Probyn said.

Diamond was starting to get angry. 'I'm doin' all

I can within the law.'

'That sounds like you've got some idea of what's goin' on,' Probyn said.

'I've got a fair idea but I can't prove it,' Diamond countered.

'Maybe I can help you prove it,' Probyn suggested.

Diamond flared up. 'I don't need no help. I work within the law, an' you don't seem like the kinda fella that does.'

'What's that supposed to mean?' Probyn demanded.

'I mean I don't want it settlin' with somebody gettin' a bullet in the back,' Diamond said. 'An' the way you wear yer iron kinda suggests that you're that kinda fella.'

Probyn looked at the sheriff. He had a past that he didn't want to talk about, but those he had shot had been facing him. They'd had a gun in their hands and he'd given them an even chance.

'I ain't no back-shooter,' he told Diamond coldly.

'That's as maybe,' Diamond said. 'But it's up to you to prove the contrary.'

'I'll prove it,' Probyn said, standing up.

'Good luck to you.'

Probyn walked along the street with a thirst growing in his mouth. He pushed his way through the batwing doors of the saloon, went up to the bar, and slammed some coins down.

'Beer,' he told the barkeep.

The barkeep filled up the glass, and pushed it in front of Probyn.

At the other end of the bar, Maxine, one of the saloon girls, watched Probyn with a predatory interest. When he had taken his first mouthful she sidled over to him.

'Looks like you needed that, cowboy,' she said provocatively.

'Sure did,' Probyn told her.

'Anyhin' else I can do fer you?' she asked him, leaning over so he could get a better view of what she had to offer.

Probyn looked her over. 'Why not?'

'Just follow me up,' she told him.

They went upstairs to Maxine's room. When she had closed the door behind her she started to get undressed.

Probyn put his beer on the small table, and started to get off his own clothes.

Soon Maxine joined him in the bed. It didn't take them long to get to it, and soon they were both breathing hard, and sweating heavily. When they had finished they both lay on the bed looking up at the ceiling.

'It sure musta bin a damn long time fer you,' she said, between rasping breaths.

'Sure was,' Probyn said, pushing aside the

memory of Abigail.'

'This yer first time in this saloon?' Maxine asked him. 'Only I don't recall seein' you round here before.'

'Only just moved into the territory. Drifted on the wind. Got myself a job at the Circle F.'

Maxine breathed in sharply. This was a surprise.

'Got to know any of the hands down there?' she asked him.

'Just a couple,' he answered. 'It's a damn fine ranch, but they're havin' a hard time at the moment.'

'Yeah, I know,' Maxine said.

Probyn suddenly remembered the time and got quickly out of bed.

'You sure soon had enough,' Maxine said, disappointedly.

Probyn had already got his pants on, and was reaching for his rig.

'Sorry' he said. 'But I've go to get back.'

'Not if you don't leave some *dinero* on the table.'

Probyn put the money on the table and left.

He rode hard to get to the ranch. When he got there Sarah was waiting just outside the house for him.

'Where the heck have you bin?' she demanded.

'Just lookin' the town over,' he told her.

'Do it on yer own time,' she said. 'Yer lucky Ransome ain't around or you might be drawin' yer money whether we're short-handed or not.'

'Won't happen agin,' Probyn told her.

'Damn right,' she replied.

Probyn looked round the yard. 'Say, where is Ransome?'

Sarah said nothing for a moment, then answered. 'Can't rightly say. Come to think of it, he ain't bin around for a spell. Bin gone almost as long as you.'

'There's a thing.' Probyn said. 'Wonder what he's up to?'

Ransome was drinking whiskey in Maitland's ranch house, along with Maitland and Spalding.

Maitland said, 'This fella's gun handy. Riley knew him down in Dodge. He had a rep for being fast out that way.'

'So how come he didn't stay out that way?' Ransome asked him.

'Dunno. I'll see if Riley can help us there,' Maitland said.

'Find out, an' if he can't help us, fix him, an' I don't want no slip-ups.'

'OK,' Ransome said, draining his glass.

Debbie was waiting in the livery stable when Ransome got back to the ranch.

'What did Maitland have to say?'

Ransome told her.

'Could be real handy,' Debbie said.

'What do you mean,' Ransome asked, puzzled.

'We could get rid of Pa, and throw the blame on Probyn,' she said coldly.

'So how are we gonna do it?' Ransome asked.

'Pa wants to go and see where the boys fixed up the fence. That means goin' through Twisted Pass. You can pick him off and send some rocks down on Probyn. Take his Winchester out of his saddle holster, and fire a few shots. That way it'll look like Probyn did it and brought the rocks down on him.'

'That way it'll look like Probyn did it,' Ransome repeated, impressed.

'That's right,' Debbie said with a bright smile. 'Ride back to Maitland's place and get it fixed up for tomorrow. I'll sort it out with Pa.'

Ransome watched as she walked to the house.

'You want to be more careful with that tongue of yours, Ransome,' said a voice behind him. 'It'll get yer neck stretched.'

Ransome's hand dropped to his .45. 'What are you talkin' about?'

'I'm talkin' about that conversation you had with Debbie, yesterday, an' the one you had just now. An' keep yer hand away from yer .45.'

'What do you want, Guthrie?' Ransome blazed at the shady ranch hand.

'I need some *dinero*, Ransome. Ain't bin havin' much luck at the gamin' tables.'

'I guess you need some cash to cover your

losses,' Ransome said, silkily.

'Yer a bright fella,' Guthrie said. 'I wuz hopin' I wouldn't have to spell it out fer you. Just somethin' else. If I have a fatal accident, like gettin' shot, I'll have left a note with the fella that runs the saloon. If you catch my meanin'.'

'I catch yer meanin',' Ransome said.

'I ain't greedy,' Guthrie said. 'Just a hundred dollars to be goin' on with. Then when Redding pays you we can have another little talk. An' nobody else need hear about it. He was drunk when I came across him in the alley by the saloon. Gettin' rid of that beer he just had. Maybe you should have a word with him? We don't want anybody else gettin' in on the gold mine. Do we?'

'I guess not,' Ransome said, tight-mouthed.

'Best be gettin' on with my chores,' Guthrie said. Ransome left the livery.

'Remember how this morning you were wanting to see the fence Miller and the others had fixed up?'

Ralph Fleming turned away from his papers. 'Yeah, honey, I remember.'

'I was thinkin'. Since you haven't been over there for a while maybe Jake Probyn could ride down with you tomorrow, and have a look at it. It would do you good. You've been looking pale over the last couple of weeks.'

Fleming thought for a minute, then looked up

31

at Debbie, who was standing beside the desk. 'I guess maybe yer right.'

'Yeah, Pa. You know I'm always thinking what's best for you.' She kissed him lovingly on his cheek, and went to tell Ransome.

She saw him coming out of the livery, looking like he could kill somebody.

'It's all fixed up, once you've told Maitland,' she said. 'I'll tell Probyn. What's the matter with you?'

'Just some trouble with one of the hands.'

'I guess you can fix it up without my help. I'm going to tell Probyn. Any idea where he is?'

'Over by the corral helping to break in one of the new horses,' Ransome said.

'I'll see you.'

When Debbie arrived at the corral she saw Probyn dusting himself off after he had been thrown from one of the horses that Ransome had bought from Mike Redding.

'Them horses ain't half-good enough for range work,' she heard him say to Miller.

'That's what I was thinkin',' Miller said. 'I wonder why Ransome bought such useless horses?'

'Beats me,' Probyn said. He went over to where Debbie was signalling him.

'What can I do fer you, Miss Debbie?' he asked her.

'Just call me Debbie,' she said, giving him an appreciative look. 'I want you to take Pa to where you fixed up that fence,' she said sweetly. 'He needs some fresh air. Tomorrow would be fine.'

'OK. Just so long as it's fine with Ransome,' he said. He wondered what was going through her mind.

'It will be, and thanks, Jake. It is Jake, isn't it?'

'Yeah, it's Jake.'

'If I can return the favour or do anything just let me know,' she said with a conspiratorial smile.

'I'll remember that,' Probyn replied.

A few hours later he saw Ransome riding out of the spread.

I wonder where that fella's going? he asked himself as Ransome disappeared up the trail.

Not long after, Ransome hauled up outside Maitland's ranch house.

'It's all fixed for ten tomorrow mornin',' he told Maitland.

'I'll get Spalding to be out there at that time. Drink?'

That night Ransome went into town to see Maxine. When they had finished sporting, Maxine propped herself up on her elbow.

'Had one of yer boys in here earlier.'

Ransome perked up pretty sharp. 'Which one of them fellas was it?'

'New fella. Jake was his name, I think.' Then she added mischievously, 'He was pretty good. So good I nearly forgot to ask him fer the money.'

33

Ransome flushed up, as if a rattler had bitten him, then he regained control of himself. This time tomorrow Jake Probyn would be buzzard meat. He ran his hand over Maxine's face.

'Sorry, hon,' he told her.

'So you should be,' she said refusing to be placated.

Ransome kissed her. 'Sorry, darlin'. That ol' man's being hard to get along with right now.'

'Maybe it's somethin' to do with the horses you were tellin' me about.'

'Yeah. Maybe it is,' he said, remembering that Guthrie would have to be dealt with before he did something crazy.

For a while they sported again, then Ransome went back to the ranch. Guthrie met him in the stable when he got back.

'Have another bad night at the tables?' Ransome asked, sensing his mood.

Guthrie gave sour smile. 'You sure know how to read a fella, don't you, Ransome,' he said sidling up to the foreman.

Ransome dug his billfold out, and opened it. 'I've only got fifty bucks on me fer now. If you want any more yer just gonna have to wait.'

'Fifty bucks will be OK to be goin' on with,' Guthrie said, taking the bills and putting them in his billfold.

'Git down to the corral and give Probyn and

them other fellas a hand.'

Guthrie slouched out of the stable and headed for the corral.

Ransome followed him out of the stable, but went in the direction of the house. Debbie was there.

'I wuz just comin' to see you,' he said. 'It's all fixed up with Maitland and his boys.'

'Glad to hear it,' Debbie said.

Ransome leaned forwards and put his arms round her waist.

'This ain't the time or the place,' she said, pulling away from him but with a smile on her lips.

'Yer right,' Ransome told her. 'See you in the livery at ten.'

She gave a throaty laugh. 'Anything you say.'

From the bunkhouse door Sarah watched them and wondered what was going on.

They finished with the horses as the light started to fade.

'OK. That's it,' Ransome said to the crew.

They broke up and headed for the bunkhouse. When he had got cleaned up, Guthrie saddled his horse.

'Wonder where he's goin'?' Loomis said. 'That's the third time this week he's bin into town. Fella's money must be burnin' a hole in his pocket.'

'At least somebody's got some money to burn a hole in his pocket.' Miller said from the other end of the bunkhouse.

Probyn watched Guthrie from the window, but said nothing.

He took the makings out onto the veranda, and built himself a stogie. For a while he leaned against the rail and watched the moon come up, then he followed Miller and Loomis down to the cook-house.

'That Guthrie must have some *dinero*.' Loomis said to Miller as Probyn sat down.

'Maybe he's got a sweetheart there,' Probyn said.

Both men snorted. 'With a face like that?' Miller said derisively.

Guthrie got to town and went straight into the Lazy Cowboy saloon.

'I still got yer note,' Wilson, the barman told him.

'Glad to hear that,' Guthrie said. 'Give me a beer.'

Wilson pulled the beer. 'There y'go,' he said. He picked up the coins that Guthrie had put down.

'Thanks,' Guthrie said, taking the head off the beer. He turned to look at the gaming tables. He sidled over and tossed the fifty bucks to the dealer.

'Fifty bucks worth of chips?' he asked Guthrie.

'Yeah, fifty bucks,' Guthrie said, picking up the chips as they were pushed across the table towards him. The play started.

There was Guthrie, the croupier, and a couple of men from town, and another individual whom nobody knew, but who had a growth of beard and looked as if he might be on the dodge. The play got hot, and the beers gave way to redeye. A couple of times the croupier tossed a glance at Wilson to see if he was around. He didn't like the way the game had started to shape up. Guthrie and the stranger were dangerously close to getting so drunk they didn't know what they were doing.

'I think it's time to close the table, fellas,' the croupier said after a hand had finished.

Guthrie looked at him. 'I'm ahead, so I say we play on.'

The croupier looked round. There was no sign of Wilson, who was big enough to take anybody.

The stranger with the growth of beard looked at Guthrie. 'The way you play, it's easy to see why yer ahead.'

'Take it easy, fella,' the croupier told him. 'I ain't seen him cheatin'.'

'He's too damn slick fer that.'

As what he was being accused of sank into Guthrie's fuddled mind the drink and the heat of the day burst into flames in his head.

'You callin' me a cheat?' he demanded lurching to his feet, and knocking the chair over. His face was beetroot-red, and his hand fell for his gun. The stranger, a bit more sober, was quicker at getting to his feet and drawing. The lead kicked Guthrie across the floor, bright-red blood bursting out of his chest.

The stranger started to back towards the batwing doors, still holding his smoking .45.

'Everybody stay where you are, or you get what he got.' He backed into the street, and across to where his horse was hitched.

Diamond was in the street, just finishing his rounds when he heard the shot.

'Hold it right there,' he shouted when he saw the man with a gun in his hand coming out of the saloon.

The gunman sobered up and turned in Diamond's direction, dragging back the hammer as he did so.

'I said hold it,' Diamond shouted again.

The gunman brought his gun up, but Diamond squeezed his own trigger. His shot threw the stranger into the dust. A minute later customers from the saloon came out into the night to get a look at the body.

'Nice work, Diamond,' Maxine said, breathless with admiration.

'Thanks, Maxine, I'll be up to collect my reward later. Now some of you people, help me git these bodies down to the undertaker's.'

He bent down to get a look at the stranger who had shot Guthrie.

'I think I got a dodger on this fella in my office,' he said.

'Either way, he shot Abe Guthrie, a hand on the Circle F,' Wilson said.

'Yeah, I knew who he was,' Diamond said. 'I'll git over there in the mornin'. It's too late now.'

Wilson went back inside, and started pulling some beers.

Diamond came into the saloon when it had finished up for the night. He went quietly up the stairs, and knocked on the door.

'That you, Diamond?' Maxine called out.

'Sure is,' the sheriff called back.

'Don't just stand out there,' she shouted. 'Get in here.'

Diamond turned the handle and went in. He recognized the excitement in Maxine's voice. It had been there the last time he had killed some-body. He knew he was in for a good time.

Across the landing, Frank Wilson was throwing off his clothes. His vest landed on the chest of drawers, then slipped off to the floor. He bent to pick it up, and noticed that the envelope had fallen out of a pocket. It was unsealed. Guthrie hadn't said what was inside it, but Wilson figured it was important.

He'd open it in the morning. Wilson folded the envelope, and put it at the back of the drawer.

FOUR

The following morning Diamond got out of Maxine's bed feeling pretty refreshed. Wilson fixed him up with ham and eggs and a heap of coffee. When he had finished, Diamond belched loudly, loosened his belt and went to check on the dodgers posters in his office. He came across a dodger that put a name to the face of the stranger he had shot outside the Lazy Cowboy the night before. Dick Fremont, bank robber. A feeling of satisfaction came over him as he scrawled out a note that he would send to the sheriff in Adlington.

He appended his name, folded it up, then walked down to the telegraph office and asked the telegraph operator to send it off. With this chore out of the way, he saddled up and rode out to the Circle F to give them the news. When he rode into the yard, Sarah was going up to the livery to check the horses.

'Hi Sheriff,' she greeted him. 'What can we do for you?'

Diamond slipped out of the saddle. and tethered his horse to the rail.

'It's about Abe Guthrie,' he said.

Sarah put her hands to her eyes, to shield them from the sun.

'Not in any trouble, is he? The boys say he didn't come back from town last night.'

'He won't ever be comin' back,' Diamond said.

'Don't matter. He was spendin' too much time in town gambling,' said Sarah.

'No, it's more serious than that. Got himself shot. He's dead.'

Sarah looked shocked. 'Shot?'

'Dick Fremont shot him. He accused Guthrie of cheatin'. They'd both bin drinking. Fremont shot Guthrie, an' I shot Fremont outside the Lazy Cowboy.'

'Are you all right?' Sarah, asked Diamond.

Diamond grinned, remembering the night with Maxine. 'Yeah, just about. I'll go an' tell your pa. You tell Ransome. He'll want to know. That's another hand you're down.'

Diamond looked uncomfortable. He felt he should have worked harder at trying to find out what was behind all the trouble. 'I'll go an' see your pa,' he said, and walked towards the house.

'Hey, Ransome,' Sarah called as the foreman

42

came across the yard.

Ransome scowled when he saw her. He'd had enough trouble trying to find Guthrie.

'Yeah, Sarah,' he said, going to meet her.

'Abe Guthrie's dead,' she told him.

Ransome felt a sudden surge of relief. Guthrie was out of the way and off his back

'What happened?' he asked.

'Got into a shootin'. Some fella reckoned he was cheatin' an' shot him, an' Diamond killed Dick Fremont outside the saloon.'

'Thanks fer tellin' me. I'm goin' to see how they boys are gettin' on with the brandin'. I'll be back in a couple of hours.'

'I'll see you later,' Sarah said as he walked away.

Ransome mounted up and headed over to Maitland's before he went to check on the branding.

'There's no need to worry,' Maitland said when Ransome got to the ranch. 'Things OK your end?'

'Yeah. The old man was about to go out with Probyn when Diamond hauled up. One of the hands got himself shot in town last night.'

'Which one?'

'Abe Guthrie.'

'The one that's got his boot on yer neck. Must be feelin' mighty pleased about that,' said Maitland.

'Sure am.' Ransome grinned. 'I've got to go an'

check on the brandin'.'

'Just make sure you don't brand any of mine,' Maitland said with a laugh.

'Sure,' Ransome said.

He had just got out of the yard when it hit him. Wilson still had the note Guthrie had written as his insurance. He dragged hard on the leathers, a cold feeling sinking into his gut. The horse slithered to a halt, and Ransome sat looking across the valley. Under his breath he cursed long and hard. Then he remembered the branding. He would think of some way of sorting out his problem later.

Jake Probyn came out of the house in front of Ralph Fleming with an uneasy feeling. Debbie didn't seem to him to be the sort of woman who would have her pa's best interests at heart. Then, he thought, as he climbed into the saddle, maybe he was just prejudiced against the woman.

Ralph Fleming was in the saddle. They crossed the yard, and passed through the gate underneath the big sign that said CIRCLE F. As they rode, Probyn kept his eyes peeled, carefully watching the ridges and the stands of trees for any movement or flash of light on the metal part of a gun.

The old man didn't have much to say. Most of the time he was quiet, as though he had lot on his mind. Probyn noticed him rubbing his eyes, and squinting hard against the sun. Even in the few days that Probyn had worked at the ranch Ralph Fleming seemed to have aged. Debbie had had to help him into the saddle, and Probyn had noticed the way she had got him up into the saddle, as if she was holding something dirty or diseased.

'We're almost there, Mr Fleming,' Probyn said as they came in sight of the fence.

'Thanks, Ransome,' Fleming said.

Probyn glanced at him. 'No, it's Jake Probyn, Mr Fleming,' he said.

Probyn glanced at the old man, and could see from the look in his face, that Ralph Fleming was near death. He reached across to prevent him falling out of the saddle. As his hand reached Fleming's saddle horn, a rifle shot blasted out of the trees some yards away. Fleming fell from the saddle. Probyn dived to the ground, scrabbling for his six-gun as another piece of lead sliced the air. He felt its hot wind passing by his cheek. He hit the ground.

Probyn could see that he couldn't help Ralph Fleming. Levelling his six-gun, he fired at the trees. A second later a piece of lead from Spalding's rifle kicked up the dirt in front of his face.

It was clear to Probyn that unless he got real lucky he wasn't going to hit whoever was taking shots at him.

Lead started to churn up the ground in front of

him. The sweat broke out on his dust-covered face, leaving wet tracks down his skin. He saw a flash of light in the trees, and took a shot at it, despite the extreme range. He heard a howl of pain, and a sense of gratification ran through him. The odds were getting better.

There were a couple more shots, then Probyn heard the sound of a horse behind him, coming up pretty fast. Then a hunk of lead passed over his head. Probyn half-turned and saw the sun shining on Diamond's star. The lawman had a smoking Winchester up to his shoulder, and was levering it as he rode.

Diamond hauled on the leathers and dropped down next to Probyn.

'Glad to see you,' Probyn said with a grin.

'Just happened to be passin' through an' I thought I'd join the party.' Diamond laughed.

'You're more than welcome,' Probyn said, pushing more loads into his .45.

There was silence, then they heard the sound of horses galloping away.

'Seems like that's it,' Diamond said. 'They get Ralph?'

'No. He just keeled over and died.'

'Damn shame. Gonna hate tellin' the girls,' the sheriff said, taking off his hat.

Both men were silent for a moment.

'We'd best be gettin' back, an' tellin' them,'

Probyn said, as they got Ralph over his saddle.

Debbie saw Probyn and Diamond coming from the house. Putting on a face of distress, she ran towards them.

'Sorry to have to do this,' Diamond said getting out of the saddle.

'What happened?' Debbie asked Probyn.

'Your pa just died. Heart gave out on him, I think,' Probyn told her. 'Then some fellas started shootin' at me. The hands can get him out of his saddle and git him into the house.'

Debbie was trying hard to look upset. 'Poor Pa. At least he didn't suffer.'

'It was quick,' Probyn said. 'Where's your sister?'

'In the house,' Debbie said. 'I'll go an' tell her.'

Probyn watched her cross the yard to the house and let herself in. A couple of the hands came out of the bunkhouse to see what was going on. Probyn watched as they eased Fleming out of the saddle and laid him on the ground.

'Damn shame,' Loomis said.

The others agreed with him.

Sarah came out of the house, her face streaked with tears. She ran to where her pa lay, and knelt down beside him, giving out a keening sound.

Probyn, Diamond and the ranch hands looked at each other. Then Probyn put his hand under her arms, and raised her to her feet.

'Get the boss into the house,' he said to the hands.

He held Sarah close to him as they took Ralph Fleming's body into the house.

Probyn looked at Sarah, and suddenly realized how much she reminded him of Abigail. Their hair was pretty much the same colour, her body had the same fresh smell that Abigail's had had, no matter what she was doing.

The ranch hands carrying Fleming's body disappeared into the house, and he guided Sarah over that way.

Ralph Fleming's body was taken into the bedroom, and put onto the bed he had shared with his wife.

'Jake,' Debbie said. 'Ride into town, an' get the undertaker to come out here.'

'Anythin' you say, Debbie,' Probyn said, easing Sarah into a chair.

Probyn saddled up, and took the trail to town. He hauled up outside the undertaker's and went inside.

'Got some business fer you,' he said to the fresh-faced kid who came out from the back.

'The fella got a name?' the kid asked, sucking on the end of a pencil.

'Ralph Fleming,' Probyn said carefully, expecting some sort of reaction.

He got one. The pencil fell out of the kid's mouth. 'Ralph Fleming?'

'You know him?' Probyn asked.

'Everybody round here knows about Ralph Fleming, and the Circle F. Them bushwhackers done fer him like they did for the others?' asked the kid, picking up the pencil and reaching for a pad.

'No, his heart just gave out, but I think the fact that we were being shot up might have had somethin' to do with it.'

The kid shook his head. 'Bad business. How are Sarah an' Debbie?'

'Sarah took it worse than Debbie,' Probyn told him.

The kid shook his head. 'That don't surprise me. Sarah an' her pa were pretty close. Debbie was a mite cold. Educated back east some place. Never liked this part of the world. Has an eye fer the fellas, like that new foreman, Ransome.'

Probyn's ears pricked up. Maybe the kid would tell him more. 'Where's he hail from?'

The kid shrugged. 'Dunno. All I know is I heard him an' ol' man Fleming arguing the last time they were in town.'

'What was it all about?' Probyn leaned on the counter.

'Somethin' about some horses Ransome had bought from Mike Redding.'

'Who's that out there, Mark?' a crotchety old voice said from behind the curtain.

The kid looked round sharply. 'Just a customer,

Mr Russell,' he said quickly.

'Maybe we can talk again,' Probyn said quietly as the curtain parted and a thin-faced old man hobbled out.

'Who's dead?' he rasped, scratching his pock-marked face.

'Ralph Fleming,' Mark said quickly.

'An' who's this fella?' Russell asked, picking at one of the scars on the side of his face.

'Jake Probyn,' Probyn said.

'An' whose Jake Probyn when he's at home?' the undertaker asked.

'Jake Probyn's a hand at the Circle F,' Probyn replied, getting nettled at the undertaker's attitude.

'Sorry if I burnt yer ass, Jake Probyn,' the undertaker said.

'Didn't you say you had to be gettin' back to the ranch?' the kid put in quickly, before Probyn lost his temper.

'Glad you reminded me,' Probyn said. 'See you around.'

Back at the Circle F Probyn hitched his horse to the rail, and went to the door. It was opened before he could knock.

'Everybody's inside,' Loomis said.

Probyn went through to what had been Ralph Fleming's office. All the hands, including

Ransome, were there, so were Debbie and Sarah; both girls were sitting under a portrait of Ralph Fleming. Sarah looked better than she had when Probyn left the ranch.

She nodded at him. Ransome scowled.

Debbie stood up. 'I guess you've heard all about my pa,' she said in a firm voice. 'I don't want any of you to worry. Things will go on as before, so I don't want anybody to worry about losing his job. As for the ranch, Pa left it equally to me and my sister.'

Probyn felt himself go cold. Here was a recipe for trouble.

Debbie and Ransome exchanged sly glances.

'We'll be burying Pa tomorrow,' Debbie said as the others digested the news. 'Till then we'd better be getting on with things. You all know what you've got to do.'

The hands left the house and went about their business.

Ransome went over to the stable and a couple of minutes later led his horse out. Probyn watched him climb into the saddle and head up the trail.

After giving him chance to get clear he went over to the hitch rail, got into the saddle and followed the foreman towards the Drowned Valley.

He watched from a rise as Ransome went into the Maitlands' ranch house.

Sure give a heap to know what Ransome an'

Maitland are talkin' about, he said to himself.

'Worked real well,' Ransome was saying as Maitland handed him a glass of red-eye.

Maitland grinned. 'All we got to do now is take care of the sister.'

Ransome sipped at the whiskey. 'I might have an idea,' he said.

Maitland's eyes screwed up. 'It had better be nothin' too obvious. Like another back-shootin' or even Jim Diamond might start takin' an interest.'

Ransome finished his red-eye and put the glass on Maitland's desk, implying that he was waiting for another.

Maitland obliged. 'Just what have you got in mind?' he asked the foreman.

'Just plannin' on sendin' her on a little holiday.' Ransome smirked.

'Just what kinda holiday?' Maitland asked, pouring himself another glass of red-eye.

'I always took a shine to Sarah, but somehow she never took a shine to me.'

'So?' Maitland raised a questioning eyebrow.

'So I know a little place just over the border, where she kin git acquainted to some *hombres*, if you catch my drift.'

Maitland laughed coarsely. 'Sure I git yer drift. It's about time she grew up a mite. What about Debbie?'

'She'll go along with it, if she knows what's good for her.'

Both men laughed.

'Best be gettin' back,' Ransome said. He drained his red-eye and stood up.

Maitland led him to the door, and they stood talking while Probyn, unseen by the pair, hauled himself into his saddle.

Ransome headed into town to see Maxine.

'Yer in a damn good mood,' she told him when they had finished sporting.

Ransome gave a laugh. 'Bin to see Maitland. We're gonna git rid of Sarah now her ol' man's out of the way.'

Maxine sat up, her chin resting on the palm of her hand. 'An' just how're you gonna do that? Another "accident"?'

Ransome turned to her. 'No, we ain't gonna kill her. Just send her over the border to spend a little time in a cathouse down there.'

'Then we'll be ready to put this ranch behind us fer good,' Maxine said.

Ransome tightened up inside. 'Yeah, we can put it behind us.'

Maxine looked at him. Something in his tone didn't ring quite true.

'OK.' She laughed as he got out of the bed and started to get dressed.

*

The morning of Ralph Fleming's funeral saw all the hands that could be spared gathered round the corral. Loomis and Miller were there, along with Probyn and Ransome. Loomis and Miller and a couple of others carried the coffin up to the small plot behind the house and lowered it in next to Fleming's wife. A short service was read over the grave.

When it was finished Ransome said: 'Back to work.'

FIVE

Ransome rode up towards Maitland's place but stopped just short of going on to it. He rolled himself a stogie and lit it, then settled back to enjoy his smoke and the sunshine. He had just about finished when the sound of hoofs got him to his feet.

'Hi, Ransome,' the driver of the wagon called to him as he got down from the box.

'Nice to see you, Mendez,' Ransome called back to the driver. 'See you managed to git a wagon. Don't want Sarah cripplin' herself on the ride down there.'

Mendez laughed. 'She ees – how you say – *bonita*? I got an *amigo* in the wagon if she is dangerous.'

'*Muy bonita*. That don't mean to say I want you fellas takin' any liberties with her until I git down there. You got that?'

'*Sí*,' Mendez said, sounding real disappointed.

'There'll be plenty of time when I get the rest of this fixed up. See you tonight near Black Rock. Till then stay outta sight.'

Ransome got on his horse and headed back to town. The saloon was pretty quiet when he got there.

'You still got that note Guthrie gave you?' he asked the barkeep.

Wilson looked at him suspiciously. 'Yeah, I got it. You want to buy it back?'

Ransome gave him a hard look. 'The hell with you, Wilson,' he rasped out sourly.

'The hell with me or not. I ain't gonna just give it to you. Reckon it's worth some *dinero*.' Wilson rubbed his thumb against his index finger.

'An' just how much *dinero* do you figure it's worth?'

Wilson looked up and down the empty bar. 'Five hundred bucks.'

Ransome swallowed hard. 'Five hundred?'

'Take it or leave it,' Wilson told him.

Ransome knew he didn't have a heap of choice. 'OK, but I ain't got it now. Yer gonna have to wait.'

'I kin wait,' Wilson told him. 'But not 'til forever.'

'Don't worry, you won't have to wait 'til forever,' Ransome told him.

He finished his beer and rode back to the ranch.

'Where have you been?' Sarah demanded when he rode into the yard.

Ransome looked round to make sure nobody was listening. 'I met this fella. He'll help us, but he don't want anybody knowing. Like a man of the law, if you know what I mean.'

'I know,' Sarah replied.

Ransome was ready to lay down his views. 'You don't sound all that convinced. Why don't you tag along? Bring yer Winchester, yer a fair shot with it.'

'Maybe we could take a couple of the boys along as well,' she said thoughtfully.

'That wouldn't be such a great idea,' Ransome said quickly. 'If our man guesses there are others along, he might decide to pull out of the deal.'

'You've made a deal with him?' she asked quickly.

'Five hundred bucks if he comes through with the goods,' Ransome told her. 'You'll have the last word on it. I've already told him.'

Sarah thought for a minute. 'OK.'

'Just remember. Don't go tellin' nobody else.' Ransome said finally.

Loomis had been watching this exchange from the inside of the livery.

That night Ransome left the bunkhouse and made his way over to the livery. As he got there Sarah came out of the shadows, looking a mite worried.

'Are you sure this is a good idea?' she challenged him.

Ransome gave her a look. 'If you don't want to go through with this, you git back up to the house, but remember what yer gonna lose.'

'OK,' she said, her voice still sounding a mite worried.

'Let's git the horses saddled,' Ransome said, guiding her into the livery.

They saddled up their horses, and headed for Black Rock. It wasn't a long ride and the night was warm.

'This is it,' Ransome said, hauling on the leathers. He slid out of the saddle.

Sarah hauled up behind him and got down. She took a look round.

'There ain't nobody here,' she said quietly.

'He'll be along,' Ransome told her.

He leaned against Black Rock and took out the makings. When he had built the stogie, he scratched a lucifer along the rock and put it to the stogie. Sarah had started to pace up and down nervously.

'Relax,' Ransome told her. 'He'll be here.'

He crushed the stogie out and listened. 'What did I say?'

Sarah turned in the direction of the approaching hoof beats.

'I thought you said there would only be one of them,' she said in a startled voice as the wagon rounded a bend in the trail.

'*Buenas tardes*, Ransome,' the Mexican driver said from the box.

'Hi, Mendez,' Ransome called back as the driver got down. 'Glad you could make it.'

'What's this?' Sarah asked in surprise.

'Just somebody to keep you company on the trip,' Ransome told her.

Sarah looked at him in surprise. 'You—' she began to say, but Ransome struck her under the chin, and she went down.

'Eet worked,' Mendez said to Ransome. 'I have an *amigo* in the back if she proves troublesome.'

'Sure it worked. Now git her tied up, and git her in the wagon.'

Mendez got his rope off the pommel and began to tie Sarah up.

Mendez and his *amigo* picked up the uncionscious girl and threw her into the wagon.

'Remember, leave her alone 'til I git down there, an' tell Fields not to put her to work 'til I git down there,' Ransome told Mendez. 'An' it won't be too long before I git over the line. I ain't stayin' up here 'til hell freezes over.'

Mendez looked at him. 'As you say, Ransome.' He turned and got mounted.

Ransome watched them go with a feeling of satisfaction. Taking hold of the leathers of his own horse, he mounted up, and rode back to the Circle F.

In the dark, he unsaddled his horse and rubbed it down. Then turned in and slept like an innocent man.

Probyn and the rest of the crew got up in the morning and started on their chores.

'Anybody seen my sister around?' Debbie asked Probyn when she saw him in the yard.

'Sorry, Miss Debbie,' he said. 'Ain't seen her all mornin'.'

'Thanks, Jake,' Debbie said, and went to look for Ransome.

'I got it fixed up. She's out of our hair, an' she won't be back fer a spell. To make it look good I'll send a couple of the hands out to look fer her,' Ransome told her. 'That horse she was ridin' wasn't the best behaved. Fair to say, he had more than a touch of the wild still in him.'

Debbie looked at Ransome. 'OK,' she said.

Ransome went off to get things organized.

'Probyn, Loomis, Miller, git yer sorry selves out an' look fer Miss Sarah. Nobody's seen her around for a while,' he said to them. 'Try Black Rock. She was headed out that way last I saw her,' he lied smoothly.

The three men got their horses saddled and headed up that way.

'That's her horse,' Loomis said as they got to Black Rock.

The horse was standing quietly chomping on the short grass.

The three men dismounted and walked quietly over to the horse so as not to spook it.

'Take a look round,' Probyn said.

The three men had a good look round. Probyn discovered the wagon tracks, but said, 'I ain't found anythin'. We'd better git back to the ranch.'

The way Probyn saw it, it wouldn't be much help to have Loomis and Miller around. If it came to gunplay they'd be a hindrance and not a help. He'd get Sarah back by himself and find out who was behind her disappearance. He thought it might be Ransome.

Miller said, 'We'd better tell Ransome about this.'

'Where did you send my sister?' Debbie asked Ransome.

'Gone to stay with some real close friends of mine in a cathouse over the border.' he said.

Debbie laughed. 'Yer a cruel fella, Ransome.'

Ransome smiled down at her, and thought that maybe she'd like to meet the same friends.

Sarah came to. Her jaw ached where Ransome had slugged her.

61

Mendez was riding up front, holding on to the leathers of the wagon. She was behind him, in the dark stuffy wagon, Mendez's *amigo* grinned at her.

'Hi,' he greeted her. 'You are feeling better, no?'

Sarah didn't answer him. She guessed she must have been out for a while. It had just gone past dawn, and they were well away from any ranches or small settlements. No help here, she thought. What the hell was Ransome's game? Why hadn't he just killed her? She was sure as hell going to kill him when she got out of this mess.

The day started getting hotter as the sun climbed up into the sky.

At last, Mendez hauled on the leathers and the wagon jerked to a halt.

'It ees time for a siesta,' he said, climbing down out of the box.

He pulled the gag out of Sarah's mouth and produced a canteen. He pulled out the stopper.

'I theenk maybe you would like some water,' he said to her.

'What d'you think, in this heat, you idiot?' she snapped at him.

His face changed and for a minute she thought he was going to slap her, then he got himself under control and put the canteen to her lips. She swallowed greedily, then he jerked the canteen away.

'Don't want you drnkin' too much. It ees bad for you out here,' Mendez said.

For a couple of hours they lay in the shelter of a rock until the sun started to go down. Then Mendez dragged Sarah into the wagon and got himself onto the box.

His *amigo* watched the whole thing in silent amusement.

'Just where are you taking me?' Sarah demanded after a while.

Mendez laughed in a way that frightened her. 'You weel soon know,' he said with a coarse laugh.

It was well into night when they got to Rio Negro.

Mendez got off the seat and knocked at the door of a house on the edge of town. Sarah could see that the house was bigger than the other houses they had passed, and there were more lights on inside. She heard Mendez knock on the door. At first the door opened just a crack.

'She ees here,' she heard Mendez say, then the door opened a mite wider.

'Git her in here, an' be damn quick about it,' she heard a man respond.

Mendez ran down the path and carried her into the house. Straight away the door was slammed shut behind her.

Sarah looked round, but didn't have time to see much.

From somewhere in the house, a woman shouted. 'What's goin' on out there?'

Sarah caught a quick glimpse of somebody dressed in shabby clothes.

'You be quiet, Maybelle, an' git back to work or you'll git another beating.'

Mendez and the other man pulled her in the direction of the staircase. They came to an open door and a flight of steps leading downwards.

There was a cellar at the bottom of the stairs. The room was well lit and there was a small bed in the corner. He tied her to the iron frame with some torn-up bed sheets.

Mendez took a step backwards. The other man leaned over her. His face was pockmarked and his breath smelled of garlic. 'You don't make a sound or you'll git the whippin' I'm gonna give Maybelle. Stay quiet an' do as yer told, an' yer stay won't be that bad. Maybe.'

Mendez came over to her 'I would do as he tells you. 'E ees a *hombre muy*—'

'Brutal,' the other man supplied. Sarah noticed that he had taken off his leather belt. 'An' just in case you wuz wonderin', I'm Jack Fields. Don't reckon you ain't heard of me, but cross me an' you'll wish you hadn't.'

He headed for the door, the belt wrapped round his fist. 'C'mon Mendez. I'll give you yer money after I've dealt with Maybelle.'

The door slammed behind them and Sarah heard them hurrying upstairs.

Probyn, Loomis and Miller were down near the chow house when Ransome came along.

'Got anythin' fer me?' he demanded.

Probyn forked another mouthful of beans into his mouth. 'Not a damn thing,' he said.

'When you've finished fattening yerself up,' Ransome said sarcastically, 'You git out an' try agin. The three of you.' He turned and walked over to the livery.

'Didn't reckon he cared all that much fer Sarah,' Loomis said.

'He don't,' Miller put in. 'He just cares about himself.'

Probyn watched as the foreman went into the livery. Ransome emerged a couple of minutes later and headed off the ranch.

'I'm gonna see where he's goin',' Probyn said to the others.

In the livery he hurriedly saddled his horse and followed Ransome at a distance. The trail led up to Maitland's place. He hitched his horse to a tree and got down in the grass so he could watch the ranch house unseen. After an hour Ransome came out. Probyn let him get clear, then followed him back to the Circle F.

Probyn let him go into the house, before riding down into the yard himself. He had almost got there when a voice called his name.

'Find anythin'?' Probyn asked Loomis and Miller.

'We found some wagon tracks,' Miller said. 'They're headed south.'

Probyn thought for a second. 'Look fellas, I don't like this. I'm gonna take a ride out there an' see if I kin see anythin' you boys might have missed.'

Loomis gave a laugh. 'Anythin' you say. We'll cover for you.'

'Thanks, fellas.' Probyn turned and headed out towards Black Rock.

He rode hard. When he got there he dismounted to look at the tracks of the wagon. Then he got back into the saddle and started to follow the tracks.

The screams of Maybelle came down from the back room to the cellar. Sarah pressed herself against the iron bedstead of the bed, feeling more and more shaky.

At last the screams stopped, but she was still shaky, imagining how Maybelle must be feeling. They must have flayed the skin off her, she thought. For a couple of minutes there was silence, then she heard someone being dragged down the stairs. A key rattled in the lock, and a crying human form was thrust into the room. Jack Fields came in. He stood over the bloody wreckage of a woman.

'That's what you've got to look forward to if 'n you misbehave,' he said venomously. 'I'm gonna leave her here so you can think on it.' He pulled the door to and Sarah heard it lock.

Pushing herself up as far as she could she took a look at the sobbing girl. Her clothes had been ripped down as far as her waist and a line of bloody welts ran across her back. The girl sobbed noisily, and her body shook as she sobbed.

'Fields sure as hell made a mess of you, Maybelle,' Sarah said angrily. 'If I get half a chance I'll kill the bastard.'

The night wore on and Sarah fell into a shallow sleep, often disturbed by the sobbing of Maybelle. In the end both she and Maybelle drifted off.

'Raise yer lazy selves,' Fields thundered, his voice wakening both girls.

Maybelle woke more slowly, but when she saw Fields, she cowered away from him into a corner at the far end of the cellar, her hands upraised to fend him off.

Fields laughed. 'Don't worry, you've had yer medicine so maybe you'll feel a whole lot better.'

Maybelle tried to press herself into the wall, and Fields laughed uproariously, his fat gut shaking as he laughed.

He looked at Sarah. 'I'll be fetchin' some vittles down presently. Don't want you fadin' away before we've had a chance to git acquainted.' He laughed again. 'An' yer admirer will be here in a couple of days to see ya.'

Sarah looked up. 'Who is this admirer?'

'Just be patient, darlin'.' He laughed and went out.

Maybelle had calmed down some and was whimpering in the corner. Sarah struggled against the torn-up sheets they had tied her to the bed with. There was no give in them.

'Can you hear me?' she said a quietly as she could to Maybelle. There was no response.

'Maybelle,' she hissed urgently. The soiled dove half-raised her head then let it drop again.

'This ain't gettin' us no place fast,' Sarah said quietly to herself.

She looked round. She called out again. Maybelle looked up. This time her head stayed up. Seeing this Sarah called out once more, and Maybelle looked in her direction.

'Over here,' Sarah hissed. Maybelle continued to stare in Sarah's direction. 'Over here, Maybelle.'

Nervously, Maybelle got to her feet, lurched over to the bed and flopped down on it. Her eyes were red and swollen with crying.

'What do you want?' she asked in a low, nervous voice.

'The same as you, I guess. I want to git outta here,' Sarah replied quietly.

Maybelle looked at her. 'There ain't no chance of that,' she whispered, looking nervously at the door.

'There's got to be some way,' Sarah persisted.

'Fields has got us all locked up, an' even if we got out of here, he's got the law in his pocket. There's no place for us to go.'

'There's got to be some place,' Sarah said impatiently.

'There ain't,' Maybelle said. 'I've thought about it a hundred times.'

Sarah was beginning to see why Fields had taken his belt to the soiled dove.

'We're still gonna have to do somethin'.'

'Such as?' Maybelle's voice was a mite steadier now.

Sarah lay back on the bed and closed her eyes. She opened them quickly as she heard a footfall on the stairs.

'Git back in the corner,' she said.

Maybelle scuttled off the bed and curled herself up in the corner. The door was unlocked and Fields came in holding a tray. 'I guess I might as well cut you loose. You ain't goin' anywhere,' Fields said to Sarah. He put the tray down. 'Got some grub fer you,' he added with a smirk.

'What about her? Don't she eat?' Maybelle said

to the owner of the cathouse.

Fields laughed. 'She eats when she's done a decent night's work.'

Sarah caught Maybelle watching Fields through her fingers. She wondered what was going through the soiled dove's mind.

SIX

Ransome was feeling pretty satisfied with himself. He'd got rid of Sarah and her old man. All he had to do was get the note Guthrie had left with Wilson, and he'd feel everything was going his way.

He walked across the yard and saw Loomis and Miller coming his way. As he saw them a thought struck him.

'Hey, you two, git over here.' Loomis and Miller turned to come his way.

'Where's yer pal, Probyn?' he asked them.

'He said he was going into town,' Miller told him.

'That's the second time this week he's bin off the spread without my say-so. He wants to draw his time or somethin'?'

'Dunno,' Miller said. 'He's a tight-mouthed fella.'

Ransome gave him a sour look. 'You know where he is?'

'Me? I dunno,' Miller said.

'You?' he asked Loomis.

Loomis shook his head.

'When he gits back, an' I mean straight away, tell him to come an' see me. OK?'

'OK,' Loomis replied.

Ransome watched them walk away, not convinced that they were telling the truth.

Wilson was in the saloon when Ransome got there that night.

'What'll it be?' Wilson asked.

'Beer,' Ransome said sourly.

'Heard you in better moods,' Wilson said, serving up the beer.

'I've bin in better moods,' Ransome said. 'What about that note?'

'What about it?' Wilson replied, wiping off the bar top. 'You know what I'm askin. I reckon it's less than what Guthrie was askin' you fer.'

Inwardly, Ransome groaned. Suddenly everybody was on his back. 'OK, but yer just gonna have to wait. Things have changed since the ol' man died. I just ain't got the money yet, but I soon will have. We've nearly got our hands on the ranch. So just wait,' Ransome told him.

Wilson smiled. 'I kin wait, so long as hell don't freeze over first.'

'Don't worry, it won't,' Ransome said. 'Say,

where's Maxine tonight?'

'Upstairs. She's got a full card,' Wilson told him.

'Guess I'll be moseyin' along then,' Ransome said, and finished his beer.

Outside, he went round the back to take a leak. He stood in the alley when he had finished and rolled a stogie. He looked up, at the rear of the saloon.

Maxine was up there, he thought. Then it hit him. Wilson's room was a couple of doors down from hers. Maybe the note was in there. If anybody saw it, he'd swing. Ransome felt his mood get darker. He looked up and down the alley. There wasn't even a cat around.

He crushed out the stogie, walked to one side of the alley and went down to the end. Quietly, he tried the latch of the yard gate. It lifted easily. He slipped inside. Above him, he could see the lights on in a back room. Maxine's. Ransome counted the windows along until he came to Wilson's. The room was in darkness and the shade was pulled down.

At the back of the saloon was a heap of old tables, which Wilson was throwing out. Ransome returned to the front of the saloon and got his rope from the saddle horn. Then he went round to the back of the saloon again.

He put two tables together and a third table on top of them. He slipped the rope off his shoulder and got onto the top table. It was pretty shaky, but less shaky than hanging.

At the side of Wilson's window a piece of timber jutted from the building. Ransome had seen it in daylight. It had looked pretty secure. He tossed the loop of the rope over it, then tested the strength of the wood by pulling on the rope. Satisfied, he started to haul himself up. When he got level with Wilson's room he reached over and swung himself so that he could brace himself against the window. He held on to the sill and pushed the window up. This done, he pulled himself into the room, hauling the free end of the rope in after him. He tied the end round the leg of a chair.

He started to move cautiously across the room, but his foot struck something, and he almost fell. Breathing hard, he stopped and listened. There was a fair amount of noise coming from the rooms of the soiled doves. He grinned and reached for the lucifers. He struck one.

'What a hole,' said to himself.

He cat-footed over to the chest of drawers and opened them, just as the lucifer burnt his fingers. Stifling a cry, he blew the lucifer out and took out another. He scraped the lucifer against his belt buckle and held it to the drawer as he opened it. Quietly, he pushed the stuff around until he found the envelope he had given to Guthrie.

Ransome took it out and put it in his vest

pocket. He blew out the lucifer. Suddenly, he sensed something and stopped.

The noise in Maxine's room had stopped. Maybe that party was over. As he started back to the window the door opened, and Wilson, holding a lamp, came into the room.

'Stand still, you bastard.' He took a step closer to Ransome. 'It took me a while to figure what you were up to.'

Ransome watched him. He was pretty shaky and looked as though he'd been drinking.

'Put the envelope on the table, an' do it real slow.' said Wilson. 'I'm going to use that as my ticket outta here.'

Ransome reached for his vest pocket. 'I guess yer gonna turn me in.'

'Why should I do that? It's like I said, that's my ticket outta here. Now put it on them drawers.'

'OK,' Ransome said, as Wilson swayed a mite.

Slowly, he put the envelope on the chest of drawers. The lamp in Wilson's hand swayed.

Ransome turned. The barkeep looked ready to drop. Ransome swung round, one hand caught Wilson on the jaw, and the other prevented the lamp from falling.

Ransome picked the envelope up again, and fed it to the lamp. He watched it curl and burn.

A groan behind him told him that Wilson was coming to.

He crushed out the flame and turned to face Wilson as he was getting to his feet.

'You crazy bastard,' Wilson shouted to him. 'The law's gonna hear about this breaking into other folk's living-quarters, an' stealin' their stuff.' He took a step towards Ransome, his face red with anger.

'So just what am I supposed to be stealin'?' Ransome asked him, waiting for the blow that he reckoned Wilson was thinking about throwing at him.

Wilson lashed out at him. Ransome sidestepped the blow and grabbed the knife in his belt. Wilson didn't see the knife and lashed out angrily again. Ransome drove the knife up to the hilt into Wilson's belly, then put his hand over his mouth to cut off any noise. Wilson slumped against him. Ransome lowered him to the floor and disentangled himself from Wilson's clutching arms.

He wiped the blade of the knife on his trousers and went to peer down into the yard. Everywhere was quiet. Slowly, he lowered himself down to the tables and headed for the gate. If anybody saw the rope, there was nothing to connect him to it.

The only other problem was Mike Redding. If Redding had told Guthrie about the horses while he was drunk, he might have told it to other folks. To be safe, he would have to silence Redding.

Ransome cat-footed up the alley. When he got to

the street, he started moving a mite faster. He climbed aboard his horse and galloped back to the ranch.

He took off his boots before going into the bunkhouse. All the hands were sleeping when he pushed the door closed behind him. With a feeling of satisfaction, he fell asleep on the bunk.

'I'm goin' over to see Mike Reddin' about these horses,' he told Debbie the next morning. 'There's no need to tell anybody where I am, if you catch my meanin'.'

'OK, Ransome,' she said. 'Just be careful. I ain't sure Reddin's to be trusted right now.'

'That's what I figured,' Ransome said, tapping his holster.

He rode over to Redding's place and stopped on the hill that overlooked the ranch. He got down from his horse and took the Winchester from the saddle boot.

The yard didn't stay empty for long. One of the hands came out of the house and walked into the livery stable. A few minutes later, he came out leading a saddled horse. Ransome levered a round into the breech of his Winchester and waited for Redding to come out of the house. The hand went back to the livery. Redding pulled himself into the saddle as Ransome raised the Winchester. The piece of lead threw Redding over the horse's back and he hit the ground on the other side. The hand came running out of the livery, but Ransome was already pushing the Winchester back into the saddle boot.

Maybelle slept restlessly, haunted by dreams of the beating that her boss had given her.

'Maybelle,' Sarah hissed in the dark.

Maybelle turned onto her side uneasily.

'Maybelle,' Sarah hissed a little louder.

Maybelle opened her eyes. 'What d'you want?' she asked, pushing herself up on one elbow.

'We've got to get outta here before you git killed,' Sarah answered.

'I know that,' Maybelle said in a weepy voice.

'We gotta stick together. I'll help you if you help me.' Sarah had sat up and was watching the door in case a light became visible.

'OK,' Maybelle said, with a little more hope in her voice. 'What you got in mind?'

Sarah said nothing. That was going to be the hard part.

'Just let me think about it,' she said quietly, straining to hear if anybody would be coming down the stairs to the cellar. 'How long d'you reckon you'll be down here?'

'Fer a spell,' the soiled dove replied. 'He don't like sendin' raw meat upstairs.'

'That's what I thought,' Sarah replied. 'You git what sleep you can.'

'Thanks,' Maybelle said gratefully.

'This ain't gettin' us no place,' Probyn said, as they hauled up near Black Rock again. The three men sat in their saddles looking out over the shimmering land.

'You sayin' we should quit?' Loomis asked him.

'No, I ain't sayin' that,' Probyn told him.

'Then what are you sayin?' Loomis asked him.

'Dunno,' Probyn answered him. 'It just seems so damned odd that all we found was her horse.'

'Me an' Loomis bin down the other side of the rock an' we ain't found her.'

'I'm startin' to think she ain't had an accident, but maybe she was kidnapped.'

Miller and Loomis exchanged glances.

'Who'd do a thing like that?' Loomis asked him.

Probyn thought hard. 'Ransome an' Debbie. That ranch was left to both sisters. Half each, so if Sarah wasn't around, Debbie would get it all.'

The other two were silent for a minute. Then Miller looked at Loomis. 'Maybe he's right,' he said.

'Only thing is I can't prove it,' Probyn said. 'I'm a stranger in these parts. What's out that way?'

'The border is a couple of days away with nothin' in between. 'Cept a couple of ranches that don't amount to much. If yer thinkin' of headin' up that way, yer gonna need some grub an' water.'

'I'd better head back to the ranch, an' pick some up,' Probyn said.

They followed him back to the ranch, and hauled up outside the bunkhouse.

Inside Probyn found the canteen of the *hombre* who had been shot just before he got to the Circle F.

'I'll fill it up,' Loomis said when Miller had gone to get some grub from the cookhouse.

He went outside to fill up the canteen. Probyn unshipped his .45 and broke it down to clean it. When he had finished, he put it together again, and loaded it up. Miller came back with a gunny-sack filled with grub.

'Got some ham an' beans, an' a hunk of bread. It'll be enough to get you to the border. An' there's a couple of small ranches that might sell you breakfast or at least somethin' to eat,' Loomis told him. 'Cookie came back, but I managed to slip a bottle of red-eye in there for you,' he added, patting the sack.

'Thanks,' Probyn said gratefully.

Miller came into the cabin. 'Time to be goin','' he said cheerfully.

Probyn got up with his stuff and went outside. He threw his stuff over the saddle of his horse and climbed into the saddle.

'See you fellas,' he said, kicking his horse's flanks and pointing him out of the yard.

He followed the trail up to Black Rock and

hauled on the leathers. The ground stretched out hard and empty under the burning sun. Tipping back his hat, he wiped away the sweat that had started to run down his face. He stretched down to reach for his canteen, then stopped. He would need that water. He touched his horse's flanks and headed for the border.

Probyn rode for most of the day, with the sun broiling him as he rode. Sweat ran down his face and neck, making his skin wet, then drying it out and chapping his face and neck. Probyn rode on without seeing anybody. At the end of the day, just as he was about to unsaddle for the night, he saw a faint glow to the west.

Pointing his horse in that direction he rode on until he reached a fence of dry, rotten wood that looked as though a good kick would send it over. Probyn rode along until he came to the gate. He slid down and opened it, then rode towards the house.

He rapped on the door and waited a while until it was opened. The *hombre* who opened it was a thin-faced individual with cold eyes. To Probyn's surprise he wore a tied-down gun. Probyn looked the *hombre* over, and recognized him for what he was.

'What can I do fer you?' he asked Probyn.

'Could use a bed fer the night, an' maybe some hot chow. I can pay.'

'Sorry, we don't take strangers in. We've had some trouble in the past few weeks.'

As Probyn was about to reply, he heard a scuffling sound behind the man, and a woman pushed her way to the door, red-faced and looking flustered.

'Sure we can offer you some hospitality fer the night,' she said. Then she stepped aside to let Probyn in. The thin-faced man was pushed out of the way, and for a second looked as if he was going to draw, then he changed his mind. 'Sorry about that,' the woman said, inviting Probyn in. 'My cousin ain't used to dealing with people.'

Probyn stepped into the cabin and looked round. There were two fellas, the woman and an older man.

The older man looked worried and his eyes kept flickering between the two men. Probyn figured something was wrong.

'Sorry about that,' the thin-faced man said.

'I figured that,' Probyn said, watching the men closely, his hand not far from his gun.

'My name's Emily Cross,' the woman said with a sweet smile. 'This is my pa, Cy,' she said pointing to the old man. 'These are my cousins, Billy and Frank.'

Neither of the cousins said anything.

'Pleased to meet you,' Probyn told them.

'We're just gonna sit down. It ain't much, but yer

welcome to a share.'

'Thanks a lot,' Probyn said, reaching for his bill-fold, and taking out a greenback.

'There's no need fer that,' Cy put in. 'Grub an' the bed's on the house.'

Emily had crossed to a pot that was hanging over the fire. She filled out the plates and handed round some eating-irons.

They sat down to eat. The two younger men ate quickly and noisily.

'You goin' far?' Frank asked Probyn.

'As far as the border, lookin' fer work,' Probyn lied.

'There ain't much work down that way,' Billy put in as the other cousin mopped up his gravy with his bread.

'There's always work down that way,' Probyn said meaningfully,

The other two seemed to relax when he said this. They threw a quick glance at each other. Probyn had figured it right. They were on the dodge, but what were they doing here? It didn't look as though Emily and Cy were the kind of folks to have anything to do with this kind of *hombre.*

The rest of the meal was finished off in silence, and then Frank started to yawn. Probyn had seen the kind of look he was giving Emily.

'Yeah, me too,' his buddy said. Both men stood up and headed for the door. Cy opened it for them and let them out into the barn where they were spending the night, which was starting to grow cold.

'There's room in back,' he said when he returned. 'It ain't big an' it ain't fancy, but it'll suit fer the night.'

'It'll be just fine,' Probyn replied.

Cy led him into the back room while Emily cleaned up the dishes.

'It ain't none of my business,' Probyn said, peeling off his rig and putting it on the bed. 'Are both them fellas related to you?'

Cy seemed scared and looked behind him at the door. 'Sorta, but they ain't the kinda relatives you brag about. In fact, they ain't really kin. It's a long story an' best left.'

Probyn took the hint and threw his shirt on the bed next to his rig. The old man left him to get some sleep. Probyn hauled off his boots and got under the thick blanket.

At first he slept deeply. Then something disturbed him, and he slowly came to the surface. The sound of voices arguing outside the room was loud and angry. He put a lucifer to the lamp. He dressed quickly and fastened on his rig.

Outside the noise was getting louder all the time. He heard Emily scream and the sound of something smashing.

Probyn ran out of the bedroom, holding the

lamp and the .45. Emily was standing by the door, her nightdress torn, and her face full of fear. Cy was getting to his feet. His hair was matted with blood. Frank and Billy were each holding a bottle of red-eye, and looking pretty drunk.

'What's goin' on?' Probyn demanded, drawing back the hammer of his .45.

'Mind yer own damn business,' Billy shouted at him, waving the bottle of red-eye at Probyn.

From the corner of his eye Probyn saw Frank go for his gun. Probyn fired. The red-hot piece of lead kicked Frank against the wall.

Billy swore and reached for his iron. Probyn's lead lifted him off his feet and slammed him against Frank's bleeding body. Emily screamed and fainted. Cy stood for a moment, not looking so great.

'You OK?' Probyn asked.

'Sure,' Cy told him. 'You sure done for them two fellas.'

Suddenly, Billy moved and groaned. Probyn fired again, then put his gun on the table. He looked at Billy.

'You ain't got long,' he said, bending down beside him.

'I know I ain't got long,' Billy said, after a long pause.

'Want me to do anythin' fer you?' Probyn asked him.

'There's damn all left fer anybody to do,' Billy gasped. 'Just one thing.'

'Sure,' Probyn said.

'In my vest pocket there's a kinda keepsake that I like to look at sometimes. I'd like to look at it now.'

Probyn reached into the pocket until he found something small and round. He took it out and gave it to Billy.

Billy looked at it for a minute, then Probyn snatched it off him.

'Where'd you git this?' he demanded of Billy.

Billy gasped and looked at him. 'Rio Negro.' he managed to gasp. 'Why?'

'I knew the girl who owned it. I don't figure she gave it to the likes of you,' he said coldly.

'No. I guess somebody like you knows she wouldn't give it to me.' Billy coughed.

Probyn grabbed him by the shirtfront and shook him. 'Tell me some more.'

'Won it in a poker game in a saloon called El Vaquero. I was just playing some fella it belonged to. I won it on the last hand,' Billy said.

'Thanks,' Probyn muttered, as Billy died. He let the cowboy's head fall gently out of his hand.

'Everythin' OK?' Cy asked Probyn.

'As OK as it's gonna be fer now,' Probyn told him.

Emily had come to and was sitting in a chair in

the corner holding a shawl round her.

'What happened?' Probyn asked Cy.

'They'd bin drinkin' an' broke the door down. Guess the were lookin' fer Emily.'

'Guess they were,' Probyn replied, his mind going back to Abigail. 'Where abouts would Rio Negro be?'

'Head due west fer a couple of days,' Cy told him. 'When you come to the river, cross it and head north. You go a couple of days, an' you'll come to it.'

'What sort of a place is it?' Probyn asked him.

Cy hesitated. 'Just a border town. Some good people an' some not so good people. From the way you wear yer gun, you'd be all right there.'

'Thanks,' Probyn said, his fingers running over the brooch that he had seen Sarah wearing.

'We'll git these fellas outside, an' in the mornin' we'll put them under before I move on.'

He and Cy dragged Frank and Billy outside and dumped them near the fence that separated a few cattle from the cabin.

'Let's catch up on some sleep,' Cy said, his chest wheezing as they got back inside. 'I'll see that Emily is OK.'

Probyn left him to it and went to bed, thoughts of Sarah and Abigail in his mind.

'That sure makes the place look better,' Cy told him the following morning when they had put the two men under.

Emily had fixed up breakfast for them. Probyn and Cy sat down to eat it. Probyn could see that Emily was looking at him with something like hero worship. It made him feel uncomfortable. He finished eating and went outside to saddle his horse.

Emily followed him to the old barn. 'You likely to be comin' back this way when you found them fellas?'

Probyn gave her a questioning look.

'You have the look of a hunter about you. Pa had the same look a while back.'

'Dunno,' said Probyn. 'It depends on how things work out. If I find who I'm lookin' fer.'

He finished saddling his horse and led it outside. Cy came out of the cabin holding a gunny-sack, which he handed up to Probyn.

'Just something' fer the trail. Emily cooked them up yesterday. They'll make yer journey more palatable.'

Probyn took the gunnysack and tied it to his pommel with the one that the boys from the Circle F had given him. He mounted up.

'Thanks,' he said looking down at them.

'Remember,' Emily told him, 'if yer ever back this way, just ride right in.'

'I will,' Probyn said with a smile. He rowelled his horse and headed up the rise. At the top he turned. Cy had gone into the cabin. Emily was still watching him.

Suddenly she gave a wave. Probyn returned the wave and rode on over the hard dry ground like that he had covered the day before.

SEVEN

Ransome had Loomis and Miller up against the bunkhouse wall. 'All right where is he?'

'Who?' Loomis asked, trying to get himself some time. It had been a couple of days since Probyn had taken off, and Ransome wanted to know where he had got to.

'Quit stallin',' Ransome said, grabbing him by the throat. He slammed him hard against the bunkhouse wall. 'Probyn, where the hell is he?'

'Dunno,' Miller said. 'We figured he didn't like the way you were talkin' to him so he hauled out an' quit.'

Ransome looked at his face for a minute to see if he was trying to be funny. 'If you see him, tell him to draw his time. He's through.'

'Gotcha,' Miller told him.

'Git this yard cleaned up, then come an' see me.' Ransome walked down to the corral and built himself a stogie. Leaning against the rails, he smoked it and thought about Probyn. He didn't figure Probyn as being the kind to ride out. He had to be up to something. He blew out the smoke and thought. Probyn might have figured out what had happened to Sarah and had maybe gone looking for her.

He crushed the remains of the stogie, got his horse out of the stable, saddled him up and rode out to see Maitland.

'So you figure he's gone to find the girl?' Maitland asked him, puffing on a heavy-looking cigar.

'Yeah,' Ransome replied, edging away from the smoke.

'I'll git a couple of boys to go after him an' put a stop to this,' Maitland said.

He tapped the edge of the cigar against the ashtray, so that a thick wedge of grey ash fell off.

'Don't know whether any of the boys told you or not. This fella's got a rep. I'll tell 'em to be extra careful.'

A couple of hours later a couple of Maitland's boys went looking for Probyn.

'Maitland figures he'll be headin' fer Rio Negro. Figures he musta heard that's where Sarah was being taken, though I can't see how.'

They hit the trail.

Maybelle was feeling a heap better and the scars on

her back had faded away.

Fields came down to look at her a couple of times. 'Git dressed,' he said to her. 'It won't be long before yer back earnin' yer keep.' He looked over at Sarah. 'Won't be long before Ransome gits down here, an' when he's sported with you, you kin start earnin' yer keep.' He gave a harsh laugh before leaving them.

Sarah crossed the room to where Maybelle was crouching on the bed.

'If he sends me back up there I don't know what I'll do. I've got to get out of here,' Maybelle wailed.

Sarah looked at her. 'OK. We'll think of somethin'. Just whereabouts are we? It was damn dark when we got in here an' I wasn't takin' a heap of notice.'

'We're in Rio Negro, the Mex side of the border.'

'Can't say I ever heard of it,' Sarah replied.

'Not a lot of folks have,' Maybelle told her.

'Whereabouts in town are we? There any law?' Sarah asked.

'Ain't any law to speak of. In fact there ain't nothin'. Outside of this place, across the street is a saloon, then a couple of shops. Out back there's a few more shops an' a church, a few houses, then it's mainly shacks that the Mex live in. Then there's the desert an' nothin' else.'

Sarah bit her lip, but said nothing. Then it hit

her. There had to be a livery stable. When they got
out of the cathouse, they'd head down to the
livery, steal a couple of horses and get out. But first
they had to get out of the cathouse.

She set her mind to working. She figured it was
morning, because the noise from overhead had
died down. It would be some time before the business of the cathouse got under way again.

'Where do yer customers come from?' she asked
Maybelle.

'We get a lot passin' trade,' Maybelle said.

'You mean outlaws and the like?' Sarah asked
her.

'Yeah, outlaws, honest folks who's found that
bein' honest ain't what it's cracked up to be, an'
just poor folks who can't make it out there any
more.'

'What's up these stairs?'

Maybelle thought for a minute. 'There's the
lounge where we meet the fellas. Then upstairs is
where we do our sportin' with them. An' Fields has
a couple of his boys, real big fellas, in case things
git outta hand. They've got rooms upstairs. None
of us girls go up there. They're a nasty pair.'

Sarah sat and thought for a minute. 'We'll make
our play tomorrow. When Fields brings our food
down, we'll jump him an' grab his gun. It'll be
quiet upstairs. First off, rip up one of yer sheets.'

Maybelle tossed her a questioning glance. 'It'll

give us somethin' to tie him up with,' Sarah told her.

Maybelle pulled a thin white sheet off her bed and started to tear it into long strips.

'Hide them strips under the rest of the sheets.'

'Sounds like a lively night,' Maybelle said after the night had started off.

Sarah was half-sitting up, supported by her elbow. 'Sure sounds it,' she said absently.

Above them the sound of hurrahing and yelling came down to the cellar. A couple of times Sarah looked across at Maybelle, She could see that she was pretty nervous, worrying about what Fields would do to her if their escape attempt failed. Sarah was worried about what he would do to *her*.

The night grew livelier, and the noise louder, until it started to slacken off.

'Get a couple of hours' sleep,' Sarah whispered to Maybelle. 'Yer gonna need yer strength fer when Fields comes through that door.'

Maybelle nodded and lay down on the bed. Sarah settled herself down and waited. A couple of times she tried to sleep, but it just wouldn't come.

She heard the footsteps on the stairs, threw back the bedclothes and shook Maybelle violently.

'It's OK,' Maybelle said. 'I wasn't asleep.'

'Fields is comin',' Sarah whispered as the key rattled in the lock.

Maybelle got herself out of the bed, and Sarah moved quickly across the room. She waited at the far side of the door. Unsuspecting, Fields pushed the door open. Sarah kicked him behind the knees and threw the blanket over his head, shutting off his screams. She grabbed the tray and brought it down on his head. He stopped struggling.

'I'll get his gun,' she told the frightened Maybelle. 'We'd best hurry an' lock him in.'

She grabbed the .45 from his holster and thrust it into her own belt. Maybelle was outside the cell and was getting ready to slam the door. Sarah took the key from the lock, closed the door and locked it.

She took a quick look up the deserted staircase. 'Let's get goin'.'

At the top she stopped and looked round. There was nobody there.

'Come on, Maybelle,' she said pointing to the front door.

The two women headed that way. As they got there one of the soiled doves came out from the sitting room, yawning, a long hank of hair hanging down her back. As soon as she saw the women she let out a yell that shook the house. Sarah smacked her good and hard across the face. The soiled dove reeled back the way she had come.

When she got to the door Sarah hesitated, then cursed. She'd forgotten about the key. Snatching the six-gun from her belt, she blew the lock off and ran into the garden. Behind her she could hear the shouts of folks in the house.

'It's them two bitches,' a voice howled.

There was the sound of running down the stairs. Sarah took a quick look over her shoulder to see if Maybelle was with her. The girl was there, and running hard.

As Sarah headed town the alley, Maybelle tried to shout something to her, but Sarah didn't hear her.

Maybelle caught up with her. 'You've come the wrong way.'

Sarah looked at her. Over her shoulder she could see the two men running from the cathouse, brandishing whips.

'They're getting awful close,' Maybelle said.

Looking round, Sarah had an idea.

'Come on, Maybelle.' she gasped. Maybelle followed her into the churchyard.

'Now what?' she asked Sarah.

Sarah ran down a path between overgrown graves until she came to the back door of a house.

'You crazy?' Maybelle snapped as Sarah hammered on the door.

A thin-faced priest opened the door. '*Sí?*' he asked.

'Sanctuary,' Sarah. said quickly, pointing to the inside of the house.

The priest, perceiving the alarm in her face, stood aside.

'It is all right. I speak good American,' he said.

'Thank God for that,' Maybelle said. Then she blushed and covered her face.

'It does not matter. God understands these things. I am Father Rico. You are in some trouble with the law?'

Sarah looked out of the window. 'Not the law exactly, Father. Just the opposite.'

Father Rico went to the window and saw the two men walking down the path, looking about them as they came.

He moved away from the window. 'Let us go into my study. They will not be able to see us there.'

The women followed him through to his small study. There was a desk covered with papers.

Father Rico pulled up two chairs. 'Sit down,' he told them. For a moment he looked them over. 'I remember you from the bordello down the street. I have seen you coming and going,' he said to maybelle. 'But you, *señorita*, I have not seen before.' He stopped speaking.

'I'm kinda new,' Sarah told him.

'And now you have some trouble, and you have come to me.'

'I didn't come down here of my own free will,' Sarah said.

Father Rico leaned forward across the table.

'Tell me what happened.'

Sarah told him.

'A very interesting story.' he said when she had finished.

'You sound as though you don't believe me,' Sarah said.

'It is, as you say, a leetle strange,' Father Rico answered.

'These ain't strange,' Maybelle said angrily She stood up and pulled off her blouse, displaying the marks of the whipping she had had.

Sarah could see the pain in Father Rico's eyes when he saw the scars.

He crossed himself quickly. '*Madre de dios.* Forgive me, *señorita.*'

'Sure,' Maybelle said, pulling on her blouse.

'How can I help you?' Father Rico asked Sarah.

'We need a couple of horses and a good head start,' she said.

'I have a *burro* at the livery stable, but I do not have a horse.'

'There'll be some down at the livery,' Sarah said, raising her eyebrows archly.

It took Father Rico a second to cotton on. He looked set to explode.

'That would be a most grievous sin,' he said.

Sarah was ready. 'Only if we ain't gonna bring them back.'

Father Rico smiled. 'I am sure God will understand, but only if you return the horses.'

Sarah and Maybelle looked relieved.

'I weel go out to the cemetery. There were men walking around out there just after you came in here. I weel go and see if they are still there,' Father Rico said. He stood up.

'Seems like we got ourselves a lucky break,' Sarah said when the priest had gone out.

'Sure hope so,' Maybelle replied. 'Sure hope so.'

When he came back Father Rico looked relieved. 'They are gone. I theenk you had better stay here for the rest of the day. Tonight I weel go down to the stable and get the attention of Manuel, the owner of the stable. He is not a God-fearing man. I hope that he weel see it as a punishment for not coming to Mass. You sneak in and borrow the horses.'

The two women spent the day catching up on some rest while Father Rico went about his parish duties.

'It is time for you to go,' he said when it was dark. He handed Maybelle an old saddlebag. 'There is water and some provisions in there, and some ointment for your back.'

'Obliged,' Maybelle said, taking the saddlebag. 'An' if yer ever down my way look me up. Won't cost you a cent.'

Father Rico blushed and Sarah gave Maybelle a shocked look.

'Sorry,' Maybelle said. 'Just wasn't thinkin'.'

Sarah grabbed her by the arm. 'Let's go.'

'*Vaya con Dios,*' the priest said.

Outside, the night was dark and heavy with the heat. They moved cautiously down the back streets until they got to the livery stable, where Father Rico put his hand on Sarah's arm.

'Stay on the other side of the street until I come to you, then hurry inside, and take the horses.'

He slipped away into the darkness. The women waited nervously.

Maybelle jumped at every sound. She knew she couldn't take another whipping.

'You OK?' Sarah asked her.

'Yeah,' Maybelle said, her voice thick and husky.

Sarah glanced at her. She sure didn't sound OK.

Then across the street a shaft of light cut into the darkness and they saw the figure of Father Rico hurrying towards them.

'C'mon,' Sarah hissed. She grabbed Maybelle's arm and hurried over to the livery.

She pushed the door open and went inside. There was no sign of the owner of the livery, but most of the stalls were occupied.

'Do you know anythin' about horses?' she asked her companion.

'I can handle one,' Maybelle told her.

'Good,' Sarah replied. She picked up some leathers and a blanket, along with a saddle.

Maybelle did the same. They climbed up into their saddles, but Maybelle found it difficult at first with having a long skirt.

'You'll git used to it,' Sarah told her with a grin.

They rode out of the livery, and headed out of town.

The two women galloped hard through the night, and as the sun started to ride the horizon, Sarah threw one hand up and dragged on the horse's leathers.

'Why are we stoppin'?' Maybelle asked in a worried tone of voice.

'Cos if we don't give them a breather they're gonna drop dead on us, an' we cain't walk fast enough to get back to the ranch before anybody catches up with us,' Sarah told Maybelle. 'Git down and git that bag opened. Take a drink of water, then pass it here.' Both women dismounted and Sarah ground-hitched their horses.

Maybelle took the canteen out of the bag and had a drink, then passed it over to Sarah.

'There's some grub in here as well,' she said with relief.

'Then hand some of it out as well,' Sarah told her.

When they had eaten Sarah said, 'How's yer back?'

'Damn sore,' Maybelle said. 'Father Rico put a tin of ointment in here.'

'If you'll pass it to me I'll put some on yer back,' Sarah offered, pushing the stopper back into the canteen.

Maybelle tossed her the tin and opened up her blouse.

'Sure made a mess of you, didn't they?' Sarah observed as she smeared the ointment over the weals.

'I can still feel the whip bitin' into me,' Maybelle said, cringing.

'Sorry,' Sarah apologized. She pushed the lid back on the tin and put it in the saddle-bag. She went to unhitch the horses.

Maybelle fixed up her blouse, then said, 'Shame Father Rico didn't put a set of pants in there as well.'

'Figure Father Rico don't know too much about female requirements,' Sarah said as she remounted her horse.

Wincing, Maybelle hauled herself into her saddle and followed Sarah.

'Them bitches must be somewhere,' Fields howled at his heavies when he realized that Maybelle and Sarah had escaped.

'Where do we start. boss?' Slater, his headman asked.

For a minute Fields glowered at him and raised the whip he had used on Maybelle. Then he got himself together. Yeah, where were they? Where could they go without some way of getting there?

'Git down to the livery, an' ask the fella down there if he knows anythin'. An' I mean ask him properly,' he said, the threat thickening his voice.

Manuel, the livery owner, was checking the horses again when Slater and another man, Gridwell, got down there.

'You lost somethin'?' Slater asked Manuel.

'Yeah, I'm two horses short.'

'Who'd they belong to?' Slater asked him.

'Some fellas from outta town. They brought them in last night.'

Slater grabbed him and shook him. 'Hope yer tellin' the truth, or Mr Fields will be askin' us to come an' see you agin.'

'I'm tellin' the truth,' the old man answered, his voice trembling. Slater and Gridwell grinned at each other, then went back to tell Fields.

'Git three horses,' Field told Gridwell, 'An' we'll get after them. They cain't have got back to the ranch yet. We'll just have to catch them up real quick. An' make sure we got plenty of water.'

Sarah and Maybelle were taking it a little slower. The desert was as hot as hell's waiting-room. If anything happened to the horses they'd be in a mess.

'This ain't gonna git no easier,' Sarah told

Maybelle, wiping the sweat out of her face.

'Just as long as they don't catch us,' Maybelle said, the fear still in her voice.

'Fields won't, even if he decides to come after us. He'd have to be damn sure which way we're headin'.'

Maybelle wasn't convinced.

EIGHT

The heat was baking everything and everyone in the desert.

'We're gonna have to stop,' Sarah said, her tongue thick and dry. They hauled on the leathers and got down. Both women looked in all directions, but there was no shade or help to be seen anywhere.

'We can't stay here all day,' Maybelle said after a while. 'We'd best be gettin' on.'

Sarah had a last look round. 'Guess yer right,' she said, and climbed back into the saddle.

They nudged the flanks of their horse and got them to walk on.

Miles behind them Fields was wondering whether going after Maybelle and Sarah had been such a great idea, but it was too late now, and he wasn't the kind of man who liked losing face in front of anybody, especially when it would mean that word would get back to the people in Rio Negro. He sure couldn't trust his heavies to keep their traps shut. Like Sarah and Maybelle, they went on in the burning heat.

'Maybe we should go back,' Maybelle said, her voice dry and thick.

Sarah twisted her head to look at the girl. 'Not after we've got this far. Besides, you know they'd kill us.'

'We're gonna die anyway,' Maybelle said miserably. 'With them it would be quick.'

'Don't you believe it,' Sarah reined in her horse. 'Men like Fields live for pain. The pain they can give others.'

She figured the beatings that Maybelle had received at the hand of Fields were really doing the talking.

'Pull yerself together,' she said. She pulled out the canteen and handed it to Maybelle. 'Don't take all of it. I want some an' it's got to last us a couple of days.'

Maybelle took a drink and handed the canteen back to Sarah. Their horses plodded on, heavily burdened with the heat.

'Looks like we're gonna get some shelter,' Sarah called out. Maybelle looked up and saw a stand of rocks shimmering some way off.

'Let's just hope it ain't no mirage.' She sounded hopeful.

'Me too,' Sarah concurred and urged her horse on.

It seemed to take all day before they got to the rocks. Sarah slid off her horse and dived for the shelter they afforded. Her horse followed her into the shade and a few minutes later Maybelle followed them in. She slumped to the ground, breathing in the cool air.

The day started to darken, and a wind sprang up. Maybelle looked up in fear.

'What is it?' she asked.

'Sandstorm,' Sarah told her as quietly as she could, but Maybelle recognizd the fear in Sarah's voice.

The wind grew fiercer and the storm more powerful. Soon it seemed as though a mob of hungry demons was trying to drag them out into the open. Sarah caught hold of Maybelle's arm and tugged it hard.

'We'll have to git up there,' she mouthed as Maybelle turned to look at her. Sarah had seen a narrow gully that seemed to offer some shelter.

Maybelle, bent double, wrapped the leathers of her horse round her hands and started after Sarah.

The wind tore at their clothes and arms; it blew their hair round their heads, and drove the sand into their mouths. Maybelle was having a hard time staying upright. Sarah grabbed at her free arm and pulled her back into the gully.

'Just stay on yer feet,' she hollered over the wind.

'I'm doin' my best,' the girl said.

They rounded a corner and straight away the force of the wind lessened, and it became very much quieter.

Both of them kneeled with their backs to the wall, using the horse as a screen to keep the wind off them. The day wore on, and eventually the wind began to slacken. Soon it was gone altogether. Sarah heaved a sigh of relief, just like Maybelle,

'Glad that's over,' Maybelle said cheerfully.

'We ain't outta the fire yet,' Sarah replied more soberly. 'We still got a ways to go, an' that water's still gotta last us.'

She felt a little of the cheerfulness go out of Maybelle.

'But don't worry too much, at least we've got rid of them cayuses. Can't see them following us in that,' she said as high spiritedly as she could.

'Could be yer right,' Maybelle replied, her spirits restored.

In the shelter of the rocks they broke open one of the food parcels that Father Rico had put up for them. They ate hungrily at the bread and cold meat.

'I feel a heap better fer that,' Sarah said when she had washed the food down with a mouthful of water.

'I feel a heap better as well,' Maybelle agreed.

For a while they rested in the rocks, until Sarah could put it off no longer. 'We've gotta be gettin' on,' she said, getting to her feet. She caught the expression on Maybelle's face.

'No good bein' like that, we've just got to push forward.

Maybelle forced a smile. 'Guess so.'

They led the horses out of the gully and mounted up, touched the horses' flanks and started out for the Circle F.

Jake Probyn had reached the edge of the storm before it got really started. He found an old ruined monastery and waited it out.

At the rear of the monastery he found a stream. He freshened himself up and filled his canteen.

He looked up into the sky and saw a couple of vultures circling. For a minute he studied them. Slowly, he let his right hand slip to his .45. He felt a cold premonition between his shoulder blades. Probyn dived to the ground as a shot rang out. His gun in his hand, he began to crawl towards the rocks from where the stream flowed. He got to the rocks and waited for the second shot. It came and ricocheted off the rocks. From the last shot, he figured that there were two gunmen. A third shot tore up the sand at the base of the rocks. He saw a shadow dart from the ruined monastery and make for some fresh cover.

Probyn took a shot at it, but he was too late, the gunman had disappeared. He looked to his left from where the second shot had come. Another shot dug out a piece of rock near his head. From somewhere just outside the monastery he heard a horse whinny. Probyn got to his feet and ran for a couple more rocks further back, hoping that the move would take the two gunmen by surprise. Probyn got there before another shot came from the two gunmen.

'You fellas asleep over there?' he called out, hoping to rile them.

He reckoned it must have worked on one of them. The next shot went wide.

'Quit that,' a voice called out.

'He's tryin' to spook you,' a voice came back.

'An' he's succeedin',' Probyn shouted back.

Another shot was even wider.

'Hope you've got a lot of water,' Probyn called out. 'Cos even if you have, yer gonna need a lot of it get you out of this desert.'

Probyn looked over his shoulder. The ruins swept in an arc beyond the rocks, and beyond that, he figured, were the horses. If he were to reach them, they would have to show themselves.

As he got to his feet and ran for it, a piece of lead kicked up the dirt behind him. 'Too late,' he called out.

There were two quick shots that didn't come anywhere near him.

Probyn looked around. He was only a few feet from the monastery and, he assumed, the horses. He ran for it. Two pieces of lead followed him. They weren't even close.

When he got into the ruins, he broke open the chamber of his gun, threw away the spent shells and loaded up again. He watched and waited. Then he made up his mind and ran through the ruins. A few yards further on he saw the horses, waiting patiently.

'If you want yer water, yer gonna have to come an' git it,' he barked.

There was silence.

Two men stepped out of the ruins. They wore their guns low and tied down. One of them looked a little shaky.

'Like I said,' Probyn told them, pointing to the horses. 'Yer water's here. Come an' get it.'

One of the men took a step forward. 'We're gonna take our water, an' it'll be over yer dead body.'

'You can sure *talk* a good fight,' Probyn replied, watching for any movement that would tell him they were going to make their play.

The shoulder of the speaker twitched as he went for his gun.

Probyn got there first. His bullet sliced open the

chest of his opponent. Then Probyn drew back the hammer of his .45, and killed the second man.

Putting fresh loads into his gun, he took a look at the dead men.

'Maitland's boys,' he said out loud.

On the other side of the desert Fields was standing over where Slater lay with a hunk of lead in him from Fields' gun.

'Get on that horse, you mangy bastard.'

'This is crazy,' Slater said. 'We just missed that storm. We ain't got any extra food or water.'

A piece of lead tore up the ground between his outstretched legs.

'Git mounted,' Fields yelled at him, his face mottled with rage.

'OK,' was the reply as Slater climbed into the saddle.

'Now, let's git,' Fields yelled.

Slater wanted to take a look behind him, but he was afraid of getting a bullet in his back. He touched his horse's flanks and pulled out. Gridwell lay a few feet away, a hunk of lead from Field's gun in him. Slater's horse was a good one. Maybe he could outrun the bullet. He knew that Fields wasn't that good a shot, putting a lot of faith in fear and his two heavies. Let Fields drift off in this heat, and he would risk it. Until then he'd let it ride.

*

Probyn felt a good deal better, having got some fresh water from the stream behind the monastery and got cleaned up. The grub that Miller had put up for him made him feel good.

Sarah and Maybelle were starting to make better time.

'Not much longer,' Sarah said in answer to Maybelle's question.

Still she scanned the horizon for any sign of help. She took the canteen off the saddle horn and shook it. There was more in it than she had expected. She hauled on the leathers and let Maybelle catch up with her.

'One good swallow,' she said and handed Maybelle the canteen.

Maybelle took a swallow and handed the canteen back to Sarah.

Probyn rested his horse and himself for a spell at noon, then went on again. Towards evening he saw a couple of dots on the horizon coming his way. He rowelled his horse's flanks and put on a spurt to see what was ahead.

Suddenly one of the dots began waving in his direction. Probyn recognized Sarah. He waved back.

'Didn't expect to see you,' he said, climbing down from his horse.

'Well, I'm glad you turned up,' Sarah said with a laugh. 'You got any spare water?'

'Sure have,' Probyn assured her and got his canteen from the saddle horn.

She took a drink and handed the canteen to Maybelle.

'This is Maybelle,' she said noticing Probyn's questioning look.

'Hi,' Probyn said.

'Hi, yerself,' Maybelle said, with some relief in her voice.

Sarah told him all about it.

'I'll get you back to the ranch,' Probyn said. He climbed back into his saddle.

'It might not be as easy as that,' Sarah told him. 'It was Ransome who fixed me up with that stay over the border.'

'I was beginning to wonder if he had anythin' to do with all the trouble you've bin havin'.'

'I can't prove it, but Debbie might be in this somewhere. Practically caught them in the stable a couple of days back,' Sarah told him.

'I ain't gonna take you straight back, not until I've got somethin' positive to hang on them,' Probyn said.

'Where are you gonna take us?' Maybelle asked.

'There's an old line shack up near Drowned Valley. A lot of the hands won't go near the place, so I reckon you'd be OK up there fer a spell.'

The two women mounted up and the trio set off for the Drowned Valley.

They got there the following night. Probyn picked out the least damaged hut and built a fire for them.

'I'll try to get back in the mornin' with some grub an' coffee fer you,' he said. Then he rode off.

Probyn rode past the ranch. He had been tempted to go into the bunkhouse and raise Loomis and Miller, but he figured it would be too risky. He might bump into Ransome, and that wouldn't be too good. He took the trail into town.

The general store was on the main street. He knew that the living quarters for the old man and his wife were above the store. They had a young man who opened up in the morning.

Probyn rode his horse round to the side of the store. He dismounted and walked along past the neighbouring buildings. There wasn't a light to be seen.

Probyn walked back to the shop and looked at the ground floor window for a moment. It wouldn't be that hard to get it open.

Opening the window was the work of a couple of seconds. Once he heard the latch snap, Probyn pushed the window up. Pushing back the curtain, he climbed silently inside. He took a lucifer out of his pocket and scratched it along his belt.

The light flared briefly for him to see what he

wanted. The lucifer flickered and died as he reached for the candles. He picked up a candle and scratched another lucifer along his belt. By its flame he lit a candle.

By candlelight he found a gunnysack and started to fill it up with what he figured Sarah and Maybelle needed.

Probyn had just finished filling it up when he heard a floorboard creak.

'Is there anybody there?' the voice sounded old and nervous.

He put the sack on the floor, and blew out the candle. From behind the door that led to the stairs, he could hear somebody coming slowly down.

The door was pushed open and an old man came in, holding a candle.

Probyn grabbed the hand holding the candle and put his free hand over the old man's mouth.

'I ain't gonna harm you,' he whispered. 'I just want some stuff from your store.'

'Just take what you want, just don't hurt me,' the old man said.

'OK, Pa,' Probyn said quietly. 'I'm just gonna have to tie you up. I won't tie you up tight. I'd appreciate it if you would give me some time to get clear before you call for help. OK?'

'OK,' the storekeeper said.

'Thanks.'

Probyn took the old man into the back room, where he tied him up pretty loosely.

He picked up the gunnysack, thought for a moment, then went back to where he had left the old man. From his billfold for he peeled off fifty dollars and put it in the old man's nightshirt pocket.

'Thanks,' he said. Then he climbed out of the window.

NINE

Probyn rode back to the Drowned Valley with the sun balancing on the horizon.

'Mornin' folks,' he said.

Maybelle was looking better. He figured she'd had a good night's sleep without the promise of a whipping. Sarah looked pretty good as well.

'Got some grub,' he told them.

'I'll fix breakfast,' Sarah said, taking the sack from him.

'Thanks,' Probyn said.

'An' what are you goin' to be doin' today?' Maybelle asked him.

Probyn smiled. 'I reckon I'll go into town an' see the sights.'

Maybelle was puzzled.

Not long after, Probyn galloped out. He made for the sheriff's office.

'What kin I do fer you?' Diamond asked stoutly,

looking up from his cup of coffee.

'Think it's about time you earned yer money,' Probyn told him. He settled himself astride the chair on the opposite side of the desk.

'What d'you mean by that?' asked the sheriff, wiping coffee off his lips.

'I mean it's about time you went out and arrested Ransome, an' a few others. Way I see it, you lean on Ransome, he'll spill the beans.'

'The hell with you, Probyn,' Diamond yelled at him.

'Take it easy,' Probyn said quietly. 'He's been up to no good and I can prove it. I've got Sarah. She'll testify against Ransome. You'll get him fer kidnappin' an' a few other things besides. I'm pretty sure Mike Redding is mixed up in it somewhere an' maybe Maitland.'

'Maitland's a respected member of this community. So is Mike Redding,' Diamond said, more evenly.

'The proof's there if you look fer it,' Probyn told him.

Diamond's hand went below the desk.

Probyn said. 'I'd cut you down before you got yer fingers round the trigger,' he said affably. Diamond knew that this was no idle threat.

'What do you say?' Probyn asked him. 'Shall we go get them?'

'There ain't a jury round here that would

believe any of it,' Diamond said. He brought his hand back where Probyn could see it.

'I guess I'll be going'. It's easy to see you ain't got no real backbone,' Probyn said acidly.

Outside he got mounted and rode off in the direction of Mike Redding's place.

'Where's yer boss?' he asked when one of the hands who seemed to be packing up his stuff.

'Gone to hell,' the hand said. Probyn dismounted.

'Diamond know about it?' he asked.

'Sure Diamond knows about it. Didn't seem overly interested.' The hand finished his packing and put his war bag on the back of his horse.

'Yer soon back,' Sarah said to him.

'Lucky to git back,' he told her. He took the mug of coffee that she offered him.

'What's the matter?' she asked.

'Mike Redding's dead,' he replied, sipping at the coffee.

'He sold Pa some horses. They weren't fit for makin' glue with. Any idea who did it?'

'Like them horses I saw in the corral? As fer who did it, my feelings lean towards Ransome,' Probyn said.

'Pa an' Redding did a fair amount of business over some horses. Pa wasn't too happy about them. He reckoned Redding and Ransome had some sort of deal goin', an' I think he might have bin right.'

Fields and Slater were making the most of their water. Slater had calmed down a mite.

'Looks like we're gonna make it,' he said to Fields.

'We'll make it,' Fields said, sounding tired. 'An' when we do I'm gonna have a long talk to Ransome. He said the whole thing would be easy. Just turn Sarah over to me, he said, an' forget all about her.'

'There's some sorta farm or somethin' over there,' Slater pointed out.

'Reckon they might spare us some water, an' maybe some grub?' Fields wondered.

The two men pushed on until they got to the low fence that Probyn had come up against.

Cy watched them from the doorway of the barn. 'You stay outta sight until we see what these fellas want,' he said to Emily. He crossed the yard as Fields and Slater came through the gate.

'What can I do fer you fellas?' he asked, keeping his hand on his gun.

'Nothin' much,' Fields said. He climbed down from his horse. Slater stayed where he was. 'Maybe you would let us fill up our canteens an' buy somethin' to fill our bellies with?'

'Yeah, there's somethin'. I'll fetch it out to you,'

Cy said, watching them closely.

He took Fields's canteen and filled it from the pump, then he took Slater's and filled that up too.

'I'll see what there is.' He walked to the back door.

Inside the cabin he found some freshly cooked meat taken from a longhorn that he had shot. He sliced it up, put it on some bread and wrapped it up. He took the packet out to Fields and Slater.

'Thanks,' Field said. He touched his hat and he and Slater rode out on to the trail.

Cy watched them go with a feeling of relief that he couldn't explain. Then he went back inside the cabin.

'It's OK, Emily,' he said 'They're gone.'

'Why'd you make me stay in here?' she asked in a puzzled tone of voice.

'Can't rightly say.' Cy shrugged his shoulders.

Probyn saw them first from the doorway of the hut where Sarah and Maybelle were hiding.

'We got some company,' he said to Maybelle.

Maybelle came to the door. Probyn saw her go white.

'What is it?' he asked her.

'Those two men. They are from Rio Negro,' she told him.

'Yer safe in here,' Probyn told her. He slipped his hand over the hammer of his gun.

Maybelle had stolen away from his side, and was cowering against the back wall. He watched as Sarah went to stand next to her. Maybelle whispered something in Sarah's ear.

Sarah hurried back to Probyn's side. She looked out of the door. Probyn saw the anger in her face. He pushed her back as she tried to run out of the hut.

'Take it easy,' he said 'You'll git yer chance. I'm gonna follow them to see where they're headed.'

When the two riders were out of sight Probyn went over to the hut where they had stabled their horses.

He got into the saddle and went after the riders, making sure that he wasn't seen.

It didn't take them long to get to the edge of the Circle F land. Fields and Slater rode down to the ranch house. From a high vantage point Probyn watched the house.

As he crouched in the long grass he heard a footstep behind him. He rose and spun round quickly, his gun in his hand.

'Hi,' Loomis said pleasantly. 'Thought we'd seen the last of you.'

'Git down,' Probyn said to him. 'I don't want anybody to know I'm here.'

'What's goin' on?' Loomis asked him.

'I'll have to tell you later,' Probyn replied. 'I want to know what them fellas are up to.'

'Things ain't so good,' Loomis whispered. 'We're still losing cattle.'

'Figured you might be,' Probyn said. He squinted down at the ranch house. 'I can't figure Fields's place in all this.'

'You ain't gonna hear a lot from here,' Loomis remarked, chewing on a long stalk of grass.

'Maybe you could help me out there,' Probyn said. 'You could ask around, quiet like. Keep yer eyes open, an' see what you can come up with.'

'You got yerself a deal,' Loomis said cheerfully.

'Just be careful, I can't see these owlhoots stopping at anythin',' Probyn warned him.

'I'll be careful all right,' Loomis promised.

Ransome watched as Fields and Slater came into the yard.

'What the hell are you doin' here,' he demanded of Fields.

Fields got down and tied his horse to the hitch rail. 'I'll tell you what I'm doin' here,' he blazed out.

Ransome looked round the yard. 'Keep yer voice down. I don't want the whole territory to know our business. We'd better go in the house.'

'Have it yer own way.' Fields followed him on to the porch.

'What's yer beef?' Ransome snapped at him.

'That little bitch Sarah. You told me it would be

a cinch,' Fields said angrily.

'So?' Ransome demanded.

'The little bitch lit out with one of my other whores, an' we're lookin' fer them.'

'I paid you enough,' Ransome told him. 'If you let her get away, that's yer damn fault. Don't come cryin' to me.'

Fields got hold of Ransome's sleeve as Ransome tried to draw his six-gun. Slater held on to Ransome's other arm.

'OK,' Ransome said. 'But she ain't bin here. Take a look round if you don't believe me.'

'All right,' Fields said, after he had calmed down. 'Where d'ya figure she is?'

Ransome thought for a minute. 'I don't know. Sarah had no friends. She spent her time lookin' after the old man, an' workin' round the place.'

'She musta gone somewhere, along with Maybelle,' Fields said. 'They couldn't have just disappeared.'

'Let me think on it fer a spell,' Ransome said.

'While yer thinkin' on it,' Fields growled, 'a splash of that whiskey would go down pretty well.'

Ransome scowled. He said nothing, but poured out a couple of glasses of Fleming's best whiskey.

The door opened and Debbie came in. 'Didn't know we had company,' she said.

'Just a couple of friends from over the border,' Ransome told her.

'Friends of Sarah's?' she asked with a cruel laugh.

'Somethin' like that,' Ransome told her.

Fields looked her up and down. She wasn't as easy on the eye as Sarah, he thought, but if they couldn't get hold of Sarah this one ould be better than showing a loss. He'd ask Ransome later.

'You had any thoughts on the matter?' Fields asked Ransome.

Ransome looked at him, but didn't answer straight off.

'I just can't think of any place,' he said slowly.

'She got no other kin round here?'

No,' Ransome said, shaking his head, and pouring a couple more whiskeys. 'Like you said, they've got to be some place. I can't trust anybody round here. I'll go an' get some of Maitland's boys and scour the territory.'

'Fine by me,' Fields said. 'We'll come with you.'

They rode out to Maitland's place.

'What can I do fer you, neighbour?' Maitland asked when Ransome and the others got there.

'Need to have the use of some of yer boys fer a while,' Ransome told him.

'What are you goin' huntin' fer?' Maitland asked when they were safely out of earshot in the ranch house.

'Sarah didn't take to life over the border. so she

came back here with a friend of hers.'

'Guess you want them found,' Maitland said.

'Got it in one.' Ransome laughed.

'I'll git some boys together,' Maitland said.

Back at the Circle F Loomis was in the stable doing some cleaning up. He had climbed into the loft and was giving himself a breather when Debbie came in and started to saddle a horse. He watched curiously through a hole in the floor.

When she had saddled the horse he crawled over to the hole and watched her ride in the direction of Drowned Valley. Loomis climbed down from the loft, saddled his own horse, and rode in the same direction, hoping to warn Probyn that trouble was on the way.

'Just what's Ransome up to?' Probyn asked when Loomis be got there.

Loomis told him.

'Looks like we're gonna have to git outta here fer a while,' said Probyn. 'I'll warn the women. You got any idea where we can wait 'til they've bin here?'

'There's a line shack, but it's on Maitland's land. Right on the edge. Just follow the trail outta here 'til you come a fork in the trail north, an' it's set on a hillside. You can't miss it.'

Probyn got the women together and they headed out for the line cabin.

*

Debbie got to the Drowned Valley just as they left. She followed them from a safe distance. When they got to the line cabin, she turned and rode back to Maitland's place.

One of the hands met her in the yard. 'You've just missed them. The boss has gone off somewhere. Took Spalding and a couple of others with him.'

'Did he say where they were goin'?' she asked impatiently.

'No,' came the answer. 'But I've got a feelin' they were headed up to Drowned Vaslley.'

Without a word of thanks, Debbie turned and rode back in that direction. After she had gone a little way she met Spalding, coming back towards Maitland's ranch.

'What are you doin' up here?' he asked.

'I've just seen Probyn an' Sarah an' some other woman headin' up to the old line shack.'

'Thanks, Debbie. I'll go up there an' fix them,' Spalding said in a satisfied way.

'Shouldn't we go and let the others know first?' she asked him.

Spalding just laughed. 'I kin take him, even though he's a fast gun. I've always reckoned I had the edge on any of them fellas.'

'Just who is this Jake Probyn?' Debbie asked him.

'Made a rep down Dodge way a while back. Got

involved with some girl. Abigail was her name. Anyways, some fella came looking fer him, an' she got caught in the crossfire. Probyn sorta disappeared after that,' Spalding told her.

'That's all the more reason fer gettin' Maitland an' Ransome and the others. Bushwhack him, an' be sure,' Debbie suggested.

'Yuh just don't get it, do you?' Spalding said to her. 'When he goes down, I'll have made my rep, an' other gunnies will be runnn' scared of me. I'll be top dog.'

'I still think it would be better if we got Ransome an' Maitland and a couple of others just to be sure.'

'Thanks fer yer concern,' Spalding said. 'I'd best be going. I don't want to miss him.'

He hauled his horse's head round and made for the line shack.

Probyn had hidden the horses round the back of the shack. He had taken his Winchester out of the saddle holster and was waiting in a stand of trees, leaving Sarah and Maybelle in the cabin.

He saw Spalding coming from a ways off. He rode as though he was in a hurry, like a man wanting to get an unpleasant chore over and done with. Probyn guessed why Spalding was in a hurry. He stepped out of the stand of trees to meet him.

'Hi, Spalding,' he said in a friendly fashion. 'Wonderin' when you'd come lookin'.'

Spalding swung out of the saddle and tethered his horse to a tree. 'The likes of you an' me got to meet some time,' he said.

'That ain't true,' Probyn replied. 'You could just get back in the saddle, an' ride out. That way we'll both be alive come sundown.'

Spalding laughed. 'We both know I ain't gonna do that, an' there's nothin' to stop you shootin' me in the back.'

'I've done some bad things, but shootin' a fella in the back ain't one of them,' Probyn said calmly.

'What about Abigail, that girl in Mason's Landin'? How come she collected some lead? That an accident, or had you had yer bellyful of her?'

'You should have ridden out while you had the chance. Now I'm gonna kill you.'

'When yer ready,' Spalding said.

A heartbeat later he was dead.

Sarah and Maybelle came running out of the shack.

'You OK?' Maybelle asked.

'Better than him,' Probyn replied, kicking Spalding's gun away from his hand.

'How'd he find us?' Sarah asked.

'Couldn't say right off,' Probyn told her. 'Somebody must have seen us comin' up here. Reckon the safest place is under their noses. If they do get there,' Probyn continued, 'some of the hands will help you if me and Loomis ain't around.'

130

TEN

Ransome was getting worried. They had ridden up to the Drowned Valley, scoured the place, and found nothing. Maitland's boys had gone back to his ranch.

Ransome waited until Debbie came back. 'What are you lookin' so pleased about?' he asked, pouring himself a glass of whiskey.

Debbie sat on the arm of his chair, took the glass from his hand, and had a drink.

'Spalding's gone up to kill Probyn,' she told him.

Ransome nearly choked. 'Where the hell is he?'

'Up on Maitland's range. Near the old line shack. Spalding's gone to kill him. All we have to do is go an' collect Sarah an' Maybelle, an' everybody's happy.'

'Git yer horse, an' we'll go an' make sure that it's Probyn who's got some lead in him.'

131

'The hell with it, Ransome,' Debbie squawked.

'The hell with you, Debbie,' Ransome bawled at her. 'We're gonna have to go up there. If it's Spalding lying in the dirt Probyn'll come lookin' fer us.'

Debbie gave him a sour look and stood up. 'I'll get the horses,' she said with a scowl.

Ransome had two more glasses of whiskey, then got up. Debbie was standing by the hitch rail, waiting for him.

'You set?' she asked him in a sulky voice.

Ransome took the leathers from her and got into the saddle. He set a hot pace up to the line cabin.

When they got there they could see that the door was open. Spalding was lying a few feet away, dried blood on the front on his shirt.

Ransome got down first and went to look at him. 'Deader than hell,' he said over his shoulder.

'I can see that,' Debbie retorted, and got down.

'So where have they gone?' Ransome snarled, his hand on his gun.

'Wherever they are,' Debbie said, 'we'd better find them before anybody else does.'

'You mean like Fields an' his buddy?' Ransome asked.

'Or maybe somebody like Jim Diamond. What we did wasn't exactly legal.'

'Diamond wouldn't believe them,' Ransome

said. 'He knows that Probyn's just a gun on the make. He'd believe nothin' that Probyn would tell him.'

'What about this Maybelle?' Debbie asked.

Ransome thought for a moment. 'She's just some whore,' he said.

'Yeah, but where are they?' Debbie asked. 'They've got to be somewhere.'

'There ain't no place I can think of right now,' Ransome said.

They rode across to Maitland's place. Maitland looked worried when they told him about Spalding. He paced up and down the room of his ranch house. 'I'll get the men out again. Them other two ain't back. An' I don't think they will be,' he said to Ransome, whose face was flushed with Maitland's whiskey. 'You git back to your place. I'll get word across there when I hear somethin'.'

Ransome and Debbie rode over to the Circle F. Ransome jumped down and hitched his horse to the rail. Debbie followed him into the house.

Ransome grabbed a bottle of Fleming's whiskey along with a glass and dropped into a chair.

'Yer gettin' a mite over fond of that whiskey,' Debbie snarled at him.

Ransome gave her a hard look and put another glassful down in one. 'Why not? I've earned it,' he snapped at her.

'We ain't outta the woods yet, not with Sarah on

the loose. An' I figure she would have told Probyn, an' I guess Probyn will have it all figured out. He's gonna come lookin' fer us.'

Ransome tossed the whiskey down. His face flushed up. 'If he comes lookin' fer us, he'll have to get past me first,' Ransome finished truculently.

'The way yer tossin' that stuff back,' Debbie said scornfully, 'yer gonna be pretty damn drunk by the time he gets to where we are.'

Ransome looked as if he was going to slap her.

'I'm goin' into town,' he yelled.

He stalked out of the house and on to the porch. His horse was still hitched to the rail. Unsteadily, he climbed into the saddle, and headed towards town.

From the bunkhouse Loomis watched him ride out. Sarah came towards him. She had seen Loomis working on the ranch a couple times, but she hadn't paid him much attention to him.

'Yer safe,' she told Loomis. 'Ransome's just ridden out, an' he just don't look so steady in the saddle.'

Loomis coloured up when he saw the way she was looking at him. It sure wasn't the way his mother used to look at him.

'Where's Jake?' she asked him in a friendly way.

He didn't figure that Jake was just going to see the soiled dove for his own pleasure. Maybe he was expecting something to happen, and he wanted to force somebody's hand, like Ransome's since it was clear that Diamond wasn't going to do anything.

Probyn had just finished his sport and had buckled on his rig when Ransome came busting into the room, still red-faced and sweating because of the whiskey.

'Probyn,' he yelled.

'Hi Ransome,' Probyn said easily. 'We're nearly ready to git the law on to you. We got Sarah somewhere safe. It's just a matter of—'

That was far as Probyn got. Maxine had got her pistol from under the pillow and hit Probyn over the head. Probyn went down without a sound.

'Nice work, Maxine,' Ransome started to say, but Maxine shut him up.

'We're gonna have to git him out of here,' she said to Ransome.

'Can't we just shoot him an' say he attacked you,' Ransome said.

'Diamond won't buy it. He comes in here for a free one sometimes, but I don't think he'll stand for murder.'

'We can't leave him here. It's payday at a couple of the ranches, an' that means I'm gonna be busy.' Ransome looked round the room, panic in his face.

'Wait here,' Maxine said.

She went to the door that led to the corridor,

and looked round, then she went briefly out into the corridor.

'Many people in the saloon?' she asked Ransome who had sobered up by now.

'Naw, it looks like they're gettin' ready for tonight,' Ransome said.

'We're gonna have to be quick an' yer gonna have to carry him.'

Ransome looked down at Probyn, who was a bit on the short side and didn't look that heavy.

'What you got in mind?' he asked.

'If we can get him in the loft we can get him out of the saloon when it closes up fer the night.'

Ransome looked doubtful.

'If you got any better ideas, just let me know,' Maxine said tartly.

'OK, but how do we get him up there?'

'When you hook this pole into the trapdoor, a ladder comes down.'

'OK,' Ransome said doubtfully.

'Git his hands,' Maxine told him.

Both of them carried Probyn out into the corridor, Maxine went to get the pole from the cupboard at the end of the corridor.

Ransome kept looking at the stairs that led down to the saloon.

Maxine fed the pole into the loop, snagged it round the door and pulled. The ladder came down.

Sweating, Ransome carried Probyn up into the loft. A minute later Maxine followed him up the ladder.

'Git him tied up, an' don't fergit to stuff somethin' his mouth.'

Then she disappeared down the ladder. A couple of minutes later she sent the ladder back up and put the pole back in the cupboard.

Ransome cut the rope into lengths, tied Probyn's hand behind him, then stuffed his bandanna into his mouth, He rested, the sweat and the whiskey running down his face. He rummaged round until he found a candle.

Its light showed that it would be a while before Probyn came to. It was going to be a long day and a long night.

ELEVEN

In the hotel down the street Fields and Slater were pacing up and down the room that Ransome was paying for.

'Any sign of Ransome yet?' Fields asked. He walked over to the window and looked down to the street.

Slater stood looking through the next window.

'I thought I saw him headin' to the saloon, but if he did go in there, he ain't come out.'

'We'll go down there,' Fields said.

They walked out of the hotel and went up the street in the direction of the saloon.

Maxine had looked out of the window and had seen Ransome's horse hitched next to Probyn's. She realized that if she didn't move the horses people would figure they were still in town.

She hurried down to the bar. 'If anybody wants

me,' she told the barkeep, 'I'll be back in five minutes.'

After making sure there were only a few people about she led the horses round to the livery.

'Al,' she said to the livery owner, 'I got a favour to ask. I want to leave these horses here fer a spell, an' I don't want you tellin' anybody about it,' she moved up close to him.

'What do I get fer it?' he asked.

'I'll give you a free one next time yer in the saloon. Honest.'

'Promise?' he said, trying to slip his hand round her waist.

'Not right now, tomorrow.' She laughed, skipping out of his reach.

Fields and Slater were just going into the saloon as Maxine disappeared round the corner with the horses.

'I thought Ransome was still upstairs with Maxine,' the barkeep replied when Fields asked about Ransome. 'She'll be back in a couple of minutes if you want to wait.'

'OK,' Fields said. 'A couple of beers while we're waiting.'

As the barkeep set them up Maxine came in.

'Couple of fellas askin' fer Ransome,' the barkeep called over to her.

'Ransome?' Maxine said innocently. 'Gone back to the ranch. He's only just gone.'

'Thanks,' Fields said, taking the top off his beer.

'Anythin' I can do for you boys,' she asked with a knowing smile.

'Some other time,' Fields said.

They watched as Maxine went up the stairs.

In the darkened loft over the saloon Ransome was starting to sweat. There was no window he could open. He looked at the still unconscious Probyn and cursed him under his breath. He finished it off with a kick to Probyn's knee. Probyn still did not move.

Fields and Slater rode back in the direction of the Fleming ranch.

'Somethin' not quite right about what that soiled dove told us,' Fields said to his companion.

They hauled on the leathers and dismounted near the spot from where Probyn had watched the ranch. They hitched their horses to a tree, then both men settled down to watch the ranch. The day wore on, and not much seemed to be happening.

'That's damned strange,' Slater said.

'What is?' Fields asked.

'That same fella who just went in there has gone in again, an' he's carryin' a tray, you know, like it had food on it.'

Fields rolled over on to his belly and spat out the stalk of grass he had been chewing. He squinted down into the yard of the ranch, just as Loomis came out.

As he left the livery, Sarah came to the door, Loomis gave her a wave and headed back to the cookhouse.

'Damn it, Sarah's in there.' Fields practically exploded.

Slater looked down. 'Bet that damn Maybelle's in there too. We gonna go down an' get them?'

Fields thought for a minute. 'That Probyn fella might be in there as well, or around somewhere.'

'We'll wait 'til it gets dark,' Slater suggested.

'Sure. They ain't goin' any place. We'll come back tonight. Maybe bring a couple of Maitland's boys along in case we need them. Now let's git back to town.'

Fields and Slater rode back to town, and went into the saloon, which was starting to fill up as the hands from the ranches drifted in to spend their money.

Slater stood at the bar, taking his time with a beer. Fields drifted into a game of poker. Al from the livery came in and went to the bar.

'Beer,' he said to the barkeep.

'Bit early in the day fer you,' the barkeep observed.

'Got somethin' to celebrate,' Al told him, taking the head off the beer.

'You come into money?' the barkeep asked

good-humouredly.

'Yer best whore, Maxine's, gonna give me a free one,' Al told him.

'Maxine knows that's against the rules. Ben'd kick her out if that wuz true,' the barkeep told him.

'Well, I'm only tellin' you what Maxine told me,' Al said.

'An' I ain't callin' you a liar, Al,' the barkeep said. 'Just that it's against the rules fer the girls to give it away.'

'The hell you ain't callin' me a liar. I did Maxine a favour with them horses, an' she'd said she'd give me one free, because I looked after them horses. That Ransome fella an' some other fella left.'

People were starting to take an interest, and they included Slater.

'OK, I think you'd better go, yer gonna cause us some trouble,' the barkeep said, pulling Al's glass away from him.

'I ain't finished yet, yuh moron,' Al protested.

The barkeep moved round the bar to get hold of Al, but Slater beat him to it.

'I'll git him outta here, an' make sure he gets to the livery in one piece.'

'On yer head be it,' growled the barkeep.

Slater got hold of Al under the arms and guided him through the crowd, who were all having a good laugh. He caught Fields's eye on the way out.

Fields folded his hand of cards and put it on the table. He followed Al and Slater out.

'What's goin' on?' Fields asked when they got out there.

'Fella reckons he's got Ransome's horse in his stable,' Slater said.

Fields' eyebrows went up. 'How've you got hold of that horse?' he asked the liveryman.

Al was beginning to realize how stupid he had been.

Fields fished out a twenty-dollar bill and gave it to Al. 'Just carry on from where you left off in the bar an' we won't say anythin'.'

Al looked doubtful, then looked at the twenty and said: 'OK, but this is just between us.'

'OK,' Fields said.

'Maxine came in with these two horses, an' she said one was Ransome's. I'd seen it before. She didn't tell me whose the other was. She said she'd give me a free one if I looked after them for a while.'

'You just show us where they are,' Fields said encouragingly.

Al took them round to his livery.

'Yeah,' Fields said, 'that's Ransome's. Don't know about the other. Thanks, fella. You don't happen to know where Ransome is?'

'No, but Maxine might know. She brought these horses in.'

'We'd better go an' ask her,' Fields said to Slater.
They turned and headed for the door.

'What about him?' Slater asked.

'If you've got yer knife with you . . .' Fields said.
'An' don't fergit the twenty.'

'Gotcha,' Slater said.

Slater came out a couple of minutes later and
handed Fields the twenty-dollar bill.

'It's OK,' Slater said. 'He won't be gettin' his
freebie or lookin' after any more horses.'

'Now we'd better start lookin' fer Maxine,'
Fields said. 'Guess the best place to start is the
saloon.'

'Yer gonna have to wait,' the barkeep told them.
'It's pay-day an' they're gettin' started early. You'd
best join the queue.'

Fields said nothing and went to find another
poker game. Slater ordered a beer, and leaned on
the bar to drink it.

After a while, the barkeep said to Slater: 'Tell yer
pal it's his turn.' Slater went to the table and said
to Fields, 'It's yer turn.' He nodded in the direction of the stairs. They had just ended a hand.

'You'll have to count me out of this hand, boys.
I got pressin' business upstairs.'

Fields asked the barkeep which room, then went
up.

Maxine was all smiles when Fields got in there.
'What'll it be?' she asked him.

144

'Just some information,' he answered, dropping the twenty dollars that Slater had retrieved for him on the bed.

'Information?' she asked, looking at the bell-rope that would get the barkeep up here if things got bad with one of her clients.

'Keep yer hands off that bell-rope. I'll kill you before you got there,' he said, drawing his six-gun.

Maxine was scared. The man looked like he meant what he said.

'What do you want?' she asked.

'Ransome, where is he?' Fields asked, fingering the .45.

'What do you want him fer?'

'You aimin' to die right now?' Fields rasped at her.

'I don't know where he is, but he'll be back here after the place closes fer the night.'

Fields watched her. She was too scared to lie, he figured. 'Keep the twenty. If he ain't here tonight, I'll kill you.' Maxine knew that he meant it.

Fields went back to the hotel with Slater. 'There's something funny going on,' he said as they walked along the street.

Maxine waited until Fields had gone, then went to the trapdoor over the corridor outside. She looked round, then got the pole and knocked on the trapdoor.

After a couple of minutes Ransome pulled the

door open and looked down.

'It ain't night yet, is it?'

'Shut up an' listen,' Maxine said to him. 'There's a fella called Fields an' another fella called Slater lookin' fer you. He's gonna be back tonight.'

'Maxine—' he said.

'It'll have to wait,' she cut in. 'I've got to git back to work,' and with that she turned and went back to her room.

Her breath was coming in sharp laboured bursts when she got there. If Ransome played her wrong after this she would kill him.

Probyn was coming to very slowly. The back of his head hurt like hell, and whatever was in his mouth wasn't helping things.

'Just keep still, Probyn,' Ransome said to him. 'Don't try anything smart or I'll kill you. Gee, I can't wait to be rid of the likes of you. When the money from that land sale comes through no one'll see me for dust.'

'How long are we gonna be here?' Maybelle asked Sarah.

She was starting to irritate Sarah. 'Hell, I don't know. A couple of days at most.'

Maybelle slouched back to the stall she had been hiding in when it looked as though Debbie was coming their way.

Debbie had gone back to the house in a rage. She had been waiting for hours for Ransome to get back, but there was no sign of him. If he'd run out on her and left her in this lousy part of the country she'd sell the ranch and spend every cent on finding him and killing him.

She poured herself a glass of whiskey and sat at her father's desk to drink it. Where the hell was Ransome?

Ransome was gloating over Probyn. 'OK, mister fast gun. You don't look so dangerous now that yer all tied up. Pretty soon yer gonna be dead, just about when Fields an' his buddy git back tonight. I might even be extra nice to Maxine. I'm just gonna run out on her. An' Debbie? She might take Sarah's place over the border. An' if I do git my hands on Sarah, a bullet will have to do for Debbie.'

Probyn was determined not to give Ransome the satisfaction of seeing him squirm.

Suddenly there was a knock on the trapdoor. He smiled to see Ransome start.

'Ransome,' Maxine called up to him.

Ransome opened the trapdoor. 'Yeah?'

'Nearly closin' time,' Maxine said.

'That's a relief,' Ransome said. 'Looks like the end of the trail, partner,' he said mockingly.

Probyn listened real hard. Through the floor-boards he could hear the opening and closing of doors, booted feet walking down the stairs.

Then everything went quiet.

A few minutes later he heard Maxine in the corridor. The ladder was let down.

'Git him down here,' he heard Maxine hiss.

Ransome picked him up as if he was no weight at all. They wrestled him down the ladder.

'Git him into my room quick,' Maxine hissed.

Ransome tossed Probyn over his shoulder and carried him into Maxine's room. The room smelled of cheap perfume, red-eye whiskey. The bedclothes looked as if they'd been in a fight.

Ransome dropped him on the bed, and took a breath. There was a half-empty bottle of red-eye on the table next to the bed. Ransome picked up the bottle and took a drink as Maxine came back into the room.

He looked at Probyn. 'Might as well take a drink. It'll be yer last.'

He took the gag from Probyn's mouth and held the bottle to it.

Probyn took the drink. It felt real good after nearly eight hours with a trail-sodden bandanna in his mouth. Probyn took a deep breath.

'He's plannin' to dump you, an' run away with Debbie,' he gasped.

Probyn could see that Maxine had been afraid of something like that for a spell.

'You lyin' bastard,' she screamed at Ransome.

'Can't you see what he's tryin' to do?' Ransome shouted back at her.

'Yer the lyin' bastard, Ransome,' Maxine shouted at him.

'He's tryin' to get us at each other's throats,' Ransome said in a more reasonable voice.

'I'm tellin' you the truth,' Probyn said. 'That's what he was always gonna do.'

Ransome made a grab for Probyn, but Maxine pushed him out of the way. He fell against the bed, and Probyn hacked at him with his boots.

Ransome rolled clear, but found himself looking at Maxine's gun.

'Stand up, you miserable sidewinder,' she said, drawing back the hammer.

Ransome got to his feet. 'Look, honey,' he said, 'I told him them things because he expected to hear them.'

'You told him them things because they were true,' Maxine said through clenched teeth. Probyn saw that the hand that held the gun was shaking.

Any time now, he thought.

Maxine's knuckles whitened on the handle of the gun. Ransome turned pale. Then somebody knocked on the door.

'Go to hell,' Maxine shouted, lowering the gun. The second she did that Ransome shoulder-charged her across the room, and bolted through the door.

The saloon owner picked himself up from the floor as Ransome disappeared down the stairs.

He stumbled into the room, and looked at Probyn.

'What the hell's bin goin' on, Maxine?' he asked. 'And who was that who went outta here.' He looked at Probyn. 'You bin givin' free ones away up here? You know I don't cotton to it.'

Probyn said, 'Get me untied. I gotta get my hands on that fella.'

Maxine unfastened his hands. Probyn picked up his six-gun and ran after Ransome.

By the time he got to the street there was no sign of the foreman.

He stood on the boardwalk for a minute, then decided that the only place Ransome could go was the ranch.

TWELVE

Probyn unhitched a horse from the rail, jumped into the saddle and rode in the direction of the ranch.

Sarah and Maybelle were still in the livery when Probyn got there.

'Where's Ransome?' he asked Sarah.

'I haven't seen him. He ain't bin here,' she said, hay still in her hair.

'What about over there?' he asked, nodding in the direction of the house.

'Don't think so,' Sarah replied. 'We ain't heard a thing 'til you got here.'

'I'm goin' down to make sure he ain't there,' said Probyn.

He strode out of the livery and down to the house. There were no lights on in the downstairs rooms that he could see. He started to hammer on the door, until eventually a light came on in an upstairs room. Probyn stopped hammering at the door until it was opened by a sleepy-looking Debbie.

He pushed past her into the corridor.

'What the hell are you doin'?' she demanded.

'I'm lookin' fer that rattlesnake, Ransome. Is he here?'

'No, he ain't here,' Debbie said to him coldly. 'Why the hell should he be?'

'Because I know what he an' you have bin up to, an' what you were gonna do with this ranch.'

'Prove it,' Debbie yelled at him.

'He told me all about it when he had me hog-tied above the saloon.'

Debbie made a lunge for the gun in the drawer of the table in the hall. Probyn backhanded her across the face, and sent her sprawling across the floor. She brushed the blood away from her lips and looked at Probyn as if he was something she'd stepped in.

'Get the hell out of this house,' she said coldly.

Probyn stood his ground. He reached across and grabbed her. 'I'll go when you tell me were I might find Ransome.'

She thought for a moment, then said 'You might find him over at Maitland's place. They're gonna run a heap of our longhorns off tonight. If yer quick, you might be able to watch. They'll be comin' at the herd from Drowned Valley.' Probyn pushed her to one side and went out again. He met Sarah and Maybelle halfway between the house and the livery.

'Git the boys out of bed, an' git up near Drowned Valley. Maitland's gonna hit the herd up there. I'll tell the night riders, though I guess they'll know by now.'

Probyn checked his six-gun, grabbed the saddle horn and swung astride his horse.

He jumped his mount over the gate and headed for Drowned Valley.

He could hear shooting before he got there.

Loomis and a couple of other boys were fighting off Maitland's boys. The longhorns were just start-ing to get restless as the shooting came nearer and nearer.

Loomis reached the edge of the herd just as the longhorns became really scared and took off, shak-ing the earth. One of Loomis's boys got himself caught in the path of the stampede. In a second his horse tried to bolt but it caught one hoof in a hole. The rider was mashed and ground into the earth before Loomis could do anything about it.

'Milt's gone,' he yelled over the noise, as another of the Circle F boys came alongside him, his six-gun in his hand.

'Yeah, I saw,' the white-faced rider said. 'Funny, ain't it?'

'What's funny?' Loomis asked him.

'Them fellas ain't tryin' to cut the beeves out. They're runnin' them to the edge of Devil's Leap. The biggest part of the herd will be lost.'

'Damn,' Loomis shouted over the rolling thunder of noise. 'You get a couple of boys an' turn them. I'll take on these rats.'

'I'll try,' the cowboy said.

'Don't try, just do it,' Loomis said. He pulled away to take on the rustlers.

Something hot just grazed the side of his head as he completed the turn. Then he came face to face with a rustler, who was levering another round into his Winchester. Loomis shot him out of the saddle.

He galloped past the stampeding herd, looking for the rustlers. A couple of times he felt the hot graze of the lead passing close to his head or body. Suddenly, two of the rustlers were stood out against the brow of a hill, their silhouettes showing briefly. Looms brought them both down.

Alongside him he heard someone shout 'Yer doin' mighty well fer a cowpoke.'

'Where have you bin?' he asked Probyn.

'I got myself tied up,' Probyn told him. 'Let's get these *hombres* finished off.'

They rode down one side of the herd then up the other side, shooting anybody they didn't recognize.

'Notice anythin'?' Probyn asked him.

Loomis thought for a minute. 'Yeah, the herd's slowin'.'

'Looks like we saved it,' Probyn said.

It was getting to dawn by the time the herd was finally settled.

'Now we've got some light we can see who these jaspers are,' Probyn said.

Loomis and Probyn started to check the bodies while the rest of the crew from the Circle F kept the herd quietened down.

'Look at who we got here,' Loomis called over to Probyn.

Probyn looked down at Maitland's body.

'That the last of them?' Probyn asked.

'Yeah, that's the last,' Loomis replied.

'There's still one missin',' Probyn said.

'Who would that be?' Loomis asked.

'Ransome,' Probyn said.

Probyn thought, as he watched the sun rise, where the hell would Ransome be?

He thought back. It was Ransome who had got Sarah fixed up to spend some time in Mexico. Now the two fellas were in town. That was where Ransome would be.

He grabbed the saddle horn and jumped aboard. Rowelling the horse he took the trail to town.

He headed for the saloon when he got there. Maxine was still in her room, looking pale and shaken. She gave him a surprised look when he walked in.

'Those two fellas that fixed up to take Sarah Flemin' to Mexico. Where are they?'

'They're stayin' in the hotel down the street. What are you gonna do?'

'I've no beef with them. It's Ransome I want.'

He walked out of the room, and went straight to the hotel.

'Mr Fields and Mr Slater. They left not long ago, with the foreman of the Fleming ranch,' the clerk told him.

Probyn dashed out of the hotel, boarded his horse, and rode for the ranch as though the devil was after him.

Ransome rode into the deserted yard of the ranch. The hands were still out, calming the steers and rounding up the strays.

Sarah and Maybelle were still hiding in the livery. Ransome rode in first, follwed by Fields and Slater.

'I'll check the house first,' Ransome told them. 'You stay here in case any of the crew git back. Yer both fast enough with them guns in case there's any trouble.'

Fields said, 'OK.' Slater said nothing.

Ransome didn't bother knocking. He went straight in.

'Glad you decided to show up,' Debbie snarled at him.

'Them other two turned up?'

'Other two? Oh, you mean Sarah an' her friend Maybelle or whatever her name is.'

'Yeah, it's them that I mean,' Ransome said. He picked up the nearly empty bottle of Fleming's whiskey, and poured what was left into a glass.

'No, they must be long gone by now,' Debbie said.

'Damn shame,' Ransome said to her. 'Fields is gonna be a disappointed man.'

Debbie looked at him. 'What d'you mean?' she asked him.

'I mean Fields is goin' to have to go back to Mexico without Sarah. Or with somebody else,' he added.

'What do you mean, somebody else?'

'Fields runs a cathouse in Rio Negro. Now with Sarah not goin' down there, an' Maybelle takin' to her heels, yer gonna have to work twice as hard.'

'Twice as hard?' Debbie echoed. Then she grasped his meaning.

Ransome was ready for her. He knocked her out with one punch.

'Slater,' he called out. 'In the livery you'll find some water skins. Fill them up an' come back here when yer ready. Fields, you come in here.'

Sarah and Maybelle had heard what Ransome said to Slater and climbed hurriedly into the loft. Slater filled the water skins and took them outside.

'We've lost the other two, but you can have Debbie instead,' he said to Fields.

Fields got a rope from Ralph Fleming's desk and tied Debbie up.

'What are you doin'?' she asked Fields as she came to.

'Yer takin' Sarah's place over the border,' Ransome told her.

'You can't do that,' she screamed.

'I can an' I'm gonna. Probyn's too hot fer me to handle, so I'm gettin' while the gettin's good. Might even come down there to see you some time, but it won't be fer a while.'

Fields heaved Debbie over his shoulder and went outside. Slater had got the water skins and was tying them to the horse.

'Have a good journey,' Ransome said to Debbie when Fields had thrown her over the horse's back.

Ransome watched them ride out of the yard. When they had disappeared up the trail he walked to his horse and took his rifle from the saddle boot and went into the house. He climbed the stairs and went into the front bedroom and across to the windows. He pushed the windows up, crouched down and scanned the yard through the sights of his rifle. Satisfied he built himself a stogie, put a lucifer to it and waited. Probyn wouldn't be long.

'What's he goin' to do?' Maybelle asked Sarah.

'At a wild guess I'd say he was goin' to bushwhack somebody,' Sarah told her.

'Ain't we gonna do somethin'?' Maybelle asked.

'Too late,' Sarah replied as Probyn came galloping into the yard. Ransome was high in the house. He crushed the stogie out, and raised the Winchester to his shoulder. As his finger curled round the trigger, Maybelle came running out of the livery.

'Look out, Jake,' she shouted.

Ransome swivelled the rifle round and shot her. The bullet caught her in the forehead, and flung her backwards. Probyn galloped through the gate, jumped off the horse and scrambled beneath the veranda.

Ransome got up from the floor and crouched against the bed, his rifle resting on the bedclothes, his finger curled round the trigger, his breathing a mite unsteady.

Probyn catfooted up the stairs until he got near Fleming's bedroom. He ignored it and went into Sarah's room.

'C'mon, Probyn. Git yours,' Ransome called out.

'I'm right here,' a voice said from outside on the balcony.

Ransome tried to turn. but Probyn shot him in the back. The impact of the bullet threw him across the bed.

Probyn went down into the yard. Sarah was bending over Maybelle, her eyes filled with tears.

'Sorry I couldn't get here any sooner,' he said quietly.

'It's OK, Jake,' Sarah said. 'We'll bury her up on the hill next to Pa.'

Not long after that the boys started drifting in. They were as Probyn had seen them on the first day he arrived at the ranch, hollowed-eyed, and dead beat.

The next day, Probyn saddled up. Loomis came out of the bunkhouse.

'I see yer leavin',' Loomis said.

'Might as well. There ain't anythin' to keep me here,' Probyn replied.

'I asked Sarah to marry me, an' she said yes. You'll be welcome at the church if yer around.'

'Thanks,' Probyn said. 'But I gotta be goin'.'

He rode out of the yard, and headed up to where Emily lived.

Funny, he thought, how she reminded him of Abigail in some ways. Maybe he'd be able to put that behind him.